Journey

to Love

Journey
to Love

LaCricia A'ngelle

www.hispenpublishing.com

Douglasville, Georgia

Journey to Love

Published by His Pen Publishing, LLC

Douglasville, Georgia 30134

Copyright ©2015 by LaCricia A`ngelle

ISBN: 978-0-9798020-8-9

Library of Congress Control Number: 2015958028

First Printing December 2015

Printed in the United States of America

10 9 8 7 6 5 4 3 2 1

This book is also available in digital eBook format

This book is dedicated to

All those that believe love is possible even if
you have to go the distance to get it.

Acknowledgments

First and foremost, I must give all praise to God. It's because of His love and the gifts He has placed within me that I'm able to share my stories with you.

To my loving family, you have sacrificed your desires and supported me allowing me to take the time to bring my stories to the world. I love you all so much and I appreciate you always. Thank you Keshonna, Larry, DeNajae, Ayonna, Gabrielle, Samantha, and my little man Landon.

To my parents Murry and Emma, thank you for believing in me. Mama, I appreciate you pushing me to birth out my dreams and visions. I know my daddy Felix is smiling down on me right now.

To my best friend Shelia, and to my readers, thank you for sticking with me. Your constant encouragement pushes me to keep going. I love you more than I can ever express in words.

I want to thank Jacquelin Thomas for mentoring me, and for the opportunity to stretch myself, and for opening up greater doors for me. Your kindness and faith in me is greatly appreciated.

Special thanks to Sean D. Young for designing my cover and my publicist Lá Tanyha Boyd,

Blessings to you,
LaCricia A'ngelle

Other Books by LaCricia A'ngelle

Girl, Naw!

Positive Deception

It Ain't Over

Available in Print and Digital format
At online retailers and bookstores

Chapter One

Christian Tyler awoke with excitement and great anticipation. His flight was booked and his plans were solidified. He was finally stepping out of his comfort zone and pursuing one of his dreams. Christian had always desired to showcase his talents in a charitable way. His company had amassed over three million in assets and he was currently working with the most efficient staff in his company's ten-year history. This would be the perfect opportunity to step away and do something for someone other than himself.

He pulled up a map on his computer and looked for Bethany, Tennessee. He was not surprised when the small town did not show up immediately. It was a rural area with a population of around three thousand according to the information given to him by project coordinators, Daniel and Deborah Joseph. Christian never imagined he would travel over nineteen hundred miles to make a charitable contribution, but he felt in his heart this was something he needed to do.

The continuous ringing of his doorbell followed by loud banging commanded his attention. The perceived urgency of the knocking let Christian know it could only be one person. He was in no rush to answer the door because he knew it would frustrate her even more.

"Good morning," he said as he swung the door open.

"To what do I owe the pleasure of your visit?"

"Don't patronize me, Christian. You know good and well why I'm here. I'm here to talk you out of this foolishness."

"What are you talking about?" He was being sarcastic. Christian knew exactly what she was talking about.

"I'm talking about this trip you're planning. It is complete foolishness, and you know it."

"It is not foolishness. I am very capable of making decisions concerning my life." Christian stepped away from the front door and headed into the living room. "I know what I'm doing."

Iris followed him into the living room and continued to berate him.

Christian gave her a hard stare. He'd had as much as he could stand. "Will you please stop trying to control my life?"

"I'm not trying to control your life. I'm simply trying to get you to understand that this move you are about to make is senseless. I don't understand why you would travel clear across the country, to a town no one has ever even heard of, to build of all things a youth center. That doesn't make any sense." Iris exhaled hard in frustration.

Pacing the floor, she waved her arms as if she was preparing to take flight. "You are known worldwide for your work. You have built homes for some of Hollywood's biggest celebrities, and who knows how many billionaires. This job is beneath you and you know it."

"I can't believe you would say something like that, especially with all that we've gone through. I worked hard to get where I am, but I give all the credit to God. I wouldn't dare allow myself to believe anything or anyone is beneath me." Christian placed his hands on top of hers and softened his voice. "This assignment will offer a much greater reward for me than any paycheck. Not everything is about money. I can't believe you are making such a big deal out of this. I travel all of the time. Why is this time so different?"

Iris snatched her hands from underneath Christian's. "Don't talk to me like I'm some kind of irrational idiot. Remember, I raised you, you didn't raise me. You may travel all of the time, but you've never been gone for that long. I'm looking out for your best interests, the same as I've done your entire life."

"I know you are, Mom. Trust me, I got this. Before I made my decision, I thought long and hard about it, and most importantly I prayed about it. I will only be gone six months to a year. Besides, with airplanes, cell phones, and Skype, it'll be just like I'm here."

"That's the other thing I don't understand. Since you want to bring up technology, you could monitor the progress from anywhere, so you wouldn't have to stay away so long. This is absolutely ridiculous."

"Mom, you know I'm a hands on man. There is no way I will have a project this big and not be there to monitor the progress. My name and reputation are something I take seriously." Smiling, Christian placed his arm around his mother's shoulder. "Now stop being difficult. You're getting upset over nothing."

Surrendering to Christian's embrace, Iris wrapped her arm around his waist and laid her head on his shoulder. "I'm going to miss you, Son. And for the record, even with all of the technology you mentioned, it's not the same as having you here."

Freeing herself from Christian's strong arms, Iris took

a seat on the couch. "Tell me about this youth center that you're getting ready to build."

With the excitement of a child, Christian's eyes lit up. He was excited to see his mother beginning to come around, but more importantly he was honored to play a part in such a worthy cause. "The name of the organization is A Mother's Love. It was founded by Daniel and Deborah Joseph." Christian joined his mother on the couch and continued his story.

"One morning during my workout, I noticed this human interest story on *Good Day Live*. The story was about a tragic car accident where the parents of five children all under the age of eighteen were killed, leaving them orphaned. There were a few family members in other states that could care for them, but none of them wanted the burden of taking in all of the children. They basically wanted to scatter them all over the country."

Settling against the back of the couch, Christian continued. "So this couple, Daniel and Deborah Joseph heard about their story, and decided to take the children and raise them as their own. Initially people thought they were crazy for taking on such a huge responsibility."

"Their pastor was a man of great influence in their community. With his support, they were able to adopt the children. This experience inspired them to start an organization for families of adopted children. A Mother's Love has grown to the point that they need a larger venue, as their church's fellowship hall can no longer accommodate the participants. This was the reason they were on *Good Day Live*. They hoped the exposure would help them to raise funds."

Puzzled and overwhelmed, Iris pressed on. "I'm

confused, how do you fit into all of this? Couldn't they have found someone in that area to build the center for them?"

"I'm sure they could have, but I want to do this," Christian stressed. "It has always been my desire to exercise philanthropy. I feel like this is exactly what I'm supposed to be doing at this point in my life. I'm not boasting, but I am one of the best contractors around."

Standing, Iris grabbed her purse off the couch and tucked it underneath her arm. "I'll admit, it's quite an impressive story. Definitely, not one you hear everyday. Taking in one child that's not even related to you can be difficult. But five, now that's quite a handful. I guess it just goes to show, not everyone is out for themselves. There are still some good people in the world."

"Yeah, there really are." Christian reached into his pants pocket and retrieved a spare key to his house. "Mom, while I'm away, I need you to come by periodically and check on things for me. I placed a hold on my mail at the post office for now. I plan to set up a temporary mailbox once I get settled in Bethany, so you won't have to worry about that. I also need you to water all of these plants you filled this place with," he teased.

Iris took the key and placed it on her key ring. "I guess I can do that for you. Shoot, I don't know how these poor plants have survived this long." She glanced up at him. "When are you leaving anyway? You still haven't said for sure."

"Monday morning," he responded. "The time there is two hours ahead of us, so I'm leaving early enough to have a productive day. You know I don't like to procrastinate. I'm going to take the weekend to tie up some loose ends before I leave."

"In that case, come by my house Sunday. I'll cook dinner for us. That way we can spend some time together before you leave."

"Sounds good, I'll be there." Christian embraced his mother, and kissed her on the cheek before escorting her to her car.

Chapter Two

Christian removed his rolling attaché case from the overhead compartment and patiently waited for his opportunity to deplane. After spending the long flight next to a snoring woman, and her obnoxious five-year-old son who could not resist kicking the back of the seat in front of him, he regretted his choice to fly coach.

Upon arriving in the baggage claim area, Christian was greeted by a young man who looked to be no more than twenty years old. The man stiffly held a small sign with *Christian Tyler* written in bold letters. He laughed under his breath at the young fella who clearly had no idea that he was holding the sign upside down.

Extending his hand, Christian greeted him with a firm handshake. "I'm Christian Tyler. You must be Landon."

"Yes, sir. It's nice to meet you, Mr. Tyler." Landon tossed his handmade sign into a nearby trash can. "Do you have more luggage to pick up?" he asked. "If so, I'll be more than happy to assist you with it."

"Yes, I do," Christian replied. "In fact, I believe I see them coming off the conveyor belt now." He retrieved two large gray and black herringbone suitcases with his initials stitched into the fabric. Years of traveling and waiting on bags taught him to invest in luggage that was not only sturdy but easily identifiable.

"I like those bags, Mr. Tyler. I've never seen anything like them. Man, and they have your initials stitched on them, too." Landon put his fist up to his mouth to exaggerate his excitement. "That luggage is tight."

Christian chuckled at Landon's excitement. "Thank you," he replied. "Trust me, when you travel as much as I do, you need something that is going to hold up."

"Let me help you with those." Landon grabbed the bags from Christian before leading him out the door. Pointing to a large parking lot across the street from the terminal, he announced, "I'm parked over there in the short term parking lot. If you want, you can stay here and I will pull the car around for you."

Christian shook his head. "I don't mind walking." Placing his hand on Landon's shoulder, he said "Look man, one thing you will learn about me is that I'm no celebrity. I don't need special treatment. I'm a regular man, just like you."

Landon nodded his head in understanding. Shrugging his shoulders, he gave Christian a sidelong glance. "In that case, right this way." He stepped quickly in the direction of his car. "Man, I like you already. We're going to get along real good."

Noticing Landon's more relaxed demeanor, Christian could not mask his laughter. "I agree."

Landon sat the luggage down next to his shiny black late model Chevy Camaro SS. Using the key fob, he pushed the trunk release button. Landon placed Christian's bags neatly inside before unlocking the car doors.

"Man, this is a nice ride," Christian complimented.

Displaying a toothy grin, Landon replied, "Thank you. It was a gift from my grandparents for my college graduation."

It was obvious to him that Landon took great pride

in his car. The interior was absolutely spotless. The dashboard and door panels shined as if they had been freshly polished. It even appeared as though Landon had gotten a fresh wash and wax prior to picking him up.

"I don't know if anybody told you this or not, but we still have about a two-hour drive ahead of us. If you want, I'll be more than happy to stop somewhere so that you can get something to eat."

"I'm not hungry right now. I had a pretty big breakfast before my flight this morning. I should be good for a while." Christian adjusted his seat belt and settled back in the seat. "Now, if you want to stop and get something for yourself, that's fine with me."

"I'm good. I stopped on the way up here and had a sandwich. Besides, I'm sure Daniel and Deborah have planned a big dinner tonight. They do it all the time when guests come in. Daniel can tear up some stuff on the grill, he always has to show off his skills." Landon licked his lips and rubbed his belly. "To be honest with you, I can't wait."

Christian grinned. "Southern barbecue, huh? I can go for some of that. I've heard Memphis has some of the best barbecue in the nation. I guess it has trickled down to Bethany."

"What! Man, Memphis ain't got nothing on us."

"Is that right? Well in that case, I'm *really* looking forward to it then."

Christian stared out of the window, admiring the thick forest and lush green fields as they traveled from Nashville to Bethany. The vegetation in Tennessee was beautiful. Various sections of Interstate 40 looked like it was hewed out of the mountains.

In an effort to make conversation, Christian spoke up.

"I take it that this is the Music Highway."

"Huh?" Landon uttered.

Realizing he must sound like a complete idiot, Christian laughed and pointed out the window. "We've passed several signs that have Music Highway printed on them. I'm sorry, I should have mentioned them when I first said something."

"Man, I thought you had some serious jetlag," Landon quipped. "That's something they started several years ago because of the deep history of music here in Tennessee. It goes from Nashville to Memphis, I believe. They have museums and everything along this stretch of highway. It's pretty cool, if you're a big music fan."

Christian pulled out his cell phone and checked his messages. He thought it was strange that he didn't have any messages, especially from his mother, but figured the time difference was the reason.

"We're pretty close to Bethany. We should be at Daniel's house in about ten minutes. I can imagine you're ready to stretch your legs. Between that flight, and this car ride, I'll bet you feel like a pretzel."

"I am a little stiff," Christian confessed, "but, I'll be all right. I'll have a chance to stretch out when we arrive."

The men continued to make small talk for the duration of the trip. Christian was happy to answer Landon's questions about Los Angeles.

Landon maneuvered his Camaro off the highway onto the exit ramp and turned left.

Christian was introduced to the town by a large white sign with the words *Welcome to Bethany* written in bold navy blue letters. He admired the tree-lined neighborhoods. Rolling down his window, he filled his lungs with the clear, southern air. The sky was a perfect hue of blue with thick, white clouds sprinkled throughout.

"This place is nice. It looks so laid-back."

"Yeah, most of the residents were born and raised here. It's a good place for families. In fact, a lot of the people that move away from here when they graduate school, end up coming back to raise their families."

Within minutes, they arrived at the Joseph family house. Landon pulled into the driveway and beeped the horn. Moving the gear shift to Park, he exhaled deeply and stretched his arms. "We're here," he said looking over at Christian. "I delivered you safely, as promised."

"Thank you, Landon. I appreciate it." Christian reached over and shook Landon's hand. "This was much better than driving from the airport in a rental car listening to computerized directions." Christian stepped out of the car and stretched his legs.

Daniel Joseph was the first to come out of the house. He stood a towering six feet five inches. Greeting Christian with a firm handshake, his large, mocha colored hands complemented his two hundred and eighty-pound frame.

"I'm so glad you were able to make it. How was your flight?"

"Everything was fine. I can't complain."

"That's good." Daniel retrieved Christian's bags from the trunk of Landon's car, and tapped the hood.

Christian presumed this was his way of giving Landon the okay to leave.

After the men waved goodbye to Landon, Daniel escorted Christian into the house.

Placing the luggage by the door, he offered Christian a seat in the living room. "Deborah will be in here in a minute. She's preparing some refreshments."

"You all didn't have to go through any trouble, I'm fine, really I am," Christian stated.

"Nonsense. It's no trouble at all. She's only preparing a light snack. I will be taking care of dinner." Daniel took a seat on the couch opposite of Christian. "We have truly been blessed by way of community support for the youth center. Everyone is delighted to have you working with us."

Sitting back against the cushions, Daniel rested one leg on top of the other, folded his hands, and placed them on top of his leg before continuing. "One of our board members owns an apartment complex that caters to business people. He has furnished apartments, and he has offered to let you stay in one for the duration of your trip."

Daniel could tell from Christian's expression he was surprised. He was hoping they would make an impression on him. He continued, "Another one of our board members is married to a car dealer. Her husband has agreed to allow you to use one of their vehicles, with a navigation system pre-installed, for your personal transportation while you are here. The best part is, neither of these gentlemen are charging us."

"Wow, that's awesome. Thank you very much." Christian could not believe the offer he was given. He was prepared to stay in a hotel, but having a furnished apartment was going to be much better. He was also delighted to hear he would have the use of a vehicle.

Deborah entered the room carrying a tray containing three glasses of iced tea, turkey sandwiches cut in quarters, fresh fruit, and mini muffins. She placed the tray on the coffee table before taking a seat on the couch next to her husband.

"Mr. Tyler, it's a pleasure to finally meet you. I can't express how much we appreciate your coming here to help us out. I'm sure there are several other projects you could be working on that offer you more money than we could ever pay."

"The pleasure is all mine," he responded, "I'm delighted to do it. When I heard your story, I wanted to participate in such a worthy project. It's nice to know there are still selfless individuals, such as yourselves, out there. These days, it seems that most people are out for themselves. For you to take on such a tremendous responsibility, raising five children you had never met is phenomenal." He leaned forward. "May I?" Christian asked gesturing towards a glass of iced tea.

"Of course, how rude of me." Deborah picked up a glass of tea, and a napkin, and handed it to Christian. She then offered a glass of tea to Daniel, before taking a glass for herself.

Christian took a mouthful of the sweet beverage. "Man, this is good. It doesn't taste like any iced tea I've had before."

Deborah smiled broadly. "Thank you, Mr. Tyler. It's actually Sun tea. It's a southern tradition."

"Sun tea… what do you mean Sun tea?" Christian didn't want to appear ignorant, but he was intrigued. "Is that a brand of tea you can only purchase here or something? I haven't heard of that." He turned up his glass, and took another gulp.

"No, I use regular tea bags. The difference with Sun tea is, you fill the pitcher with cold water and tea bags, then you sit it out in the sun until the tea reaches full strength.

It usually takes several hours, depending on how hot it is outside and how much the sun is shining. The more direct sunlight you have the better." Deborah sat back on the couch and rubbed her husband's knee. "I usually set the tea out early in the morning, and leave it until the afternoon. The slow brewing gives it a better taste in my opinion."

Daniel placed his arm around Deborah's shoulder. "Sweetheart, you are going to talk the poor man's ear off." After polishing off the remnants of his tea, he turned his attention back to Christian.

"I know you came prepared to work today, but I don't think it would be fair to have you come so far, and not allow you to rest up a little. We're planning a cookout later this evening. You wouldn't believe how many people are eager to meet you."

Daniel removed his arm from Deborah's shoulder and clasped his hands together. "Tell you what, why don't I take you to get the car, and then I will show you to the apartment. You can have some time to get settled in, and then I'll come by in a few hours to get you for the cookout."

Christian quickly agreed. Fatigue from his trip was starting to set in and he welcomed the idea of resting up before the festivities. He also needed to call his mother and to contact his business associates, to make them aware of his arrival. Iris was sure to be worried if he took too much longer calling her. Being the only child, he was used to his mother being over protective. Deborah offered to wrap the sandwiches she had prepared up for Christian before Daniel whisked him off.

Daniel chose to take Christian to the car dealership first. Christian's lips curved up into a wide grin when he received the keys to a charcoal gray Toyota Avalon.

The car offered top of the line amenities, which included heated and air conditioned leather seats, a sunroof, and satellite radio. The owner of the dealership repeatedly expressed his gratitude for Christian taking on the youth center project. He was one of several local sponsors for the building construction.

After picking up the car, Christian followed Daniel to the apartment complex where he would be staying. Christian surveyed his surroundings. A large flagpole in the center of the courtyard was surrounded by tulips in various colors. The grounds were beautifully landscaped with manicured lawns and thick green shrubs garnished with red mulch. The complex contained three separate brick buildings. Each building housed its own fitness center. The buildings were two stories high with private balconies outside of each apartment.

Daniel introduced him to the building manager, who in turn showed him to his apartment. An enclosed staircase gave them access to the second floor where Christian's apartment was located. The manager opened the door for Christian before presenting him with the key. "It's a pleasure meeting you, Mr. Tyler. We hope you will enjoy your stay with us. If you need anything, the office phone number is located on a card in the kitchen. Feel free to give us a call anytime." He then excused himself, leaving Christian and Daniel alone in the apartment.

"I'm going to leave so that you can get settled in. I'll give you a call in a few hours and you can decide if you want us to come back and get you, or if you'd like to drive over on your own. If you need anything, please don't hesitate to call."

"Thanks again for everything. I'm looking forward to

working with you and your family." Christian shook Daniel's hand and walked him to the door.

He placed his bags inside the closet located by the front door before touring the apartment. Next to the closet was a laundry room equipped with a washer and dryer. To his immediate left, there was a small fully equipped kitchen complete with dishes. On the other side of the open kitchen was a small dining area, furnished with a round glass table and four plush camel colored chairs. The living room contained a chocolate brown sofa and love seat with thick camel colored cushions. The wall opposite the couch held a large flat screen high definition television with a built in Blu-ray player and satellite TV.

The bedroom contained an oak king-sized sleigh bed with matching nightstands. An oversized dark brown recliner sat in the corner of the room. Across from the bed, a smaller, flat-screen television was mounted on the wall above a chest of drawers. A walk-in closet connected the bedroom to the bathroom. The bathroom also had a separate entrance located next to the laundry room.

He couldn't believe his eyes. An apartment like this would easily go for sixteen hundred dollars a month in L.A. He was going to have to ask Daniel how much the rent was. Given the location, he figured it would be significantly lower.

Without any further hesitation, Christian pulled out his cell phone and gave voice instruction to call his mother. When the call failed to connect he realized it was still in airplane mode. He adjusted the settings and attempted his call again.

After a few short rings Iris picked up.

"It's about time you called, I was worried sick. I tried

calling you, but your phone went straight to voicemail. I have been watching the news and everything, I stopped short of calling the airport to see if they'd had a plane to crash. I can't believe you didn't even text me or anything."

"You always get yourself all worked up over nothing. I'm fine. I'd forgotten to take my phone off airplane mode. Following my flight, I had a two-hour car ride to Bethany. But, I'm here now." He knew he wouldn't win a debate with his mother, so he surrendered. "I apologize for keeping you waiting. I should have at least texted you."

Christian walked over to the cabinet and removed a glass. He rinsed it out, before moving over to the double sided refrigerator and filling the glass with crushed ice and water. "Ma, you won't believe what all has happened to me since I arrived. Once I made it to Bethany, I met Daniel and his wife Deborah. She made Sun tea, which was pretty good; I'll have to tell you more about that later. Anyway, they gave me a brand new Toyota Avalon to drive while I'm here, which didn't cost me anything might I add. It's even equipped with a navigation system, so I don't have to depend on anybody to get me where I need to go."

Iris couldn't help but to be sarcastic. "That's the least they could do. You are losing a lot of money being there."

"Come on, Mom, let it go." Christian took a deep cleansing breath before continuing. "In addition to the car, they put me up in a completely furnished apartment which is much better than a hotel room. This apartment has everything too, including a laundry room which is great. You know how much I hate Laundromats. Did I mention the apartment is also rent free? It looks like they have a lot of support for the youth center project. The car and apartment were courtesy of some of the board members."

"That's good, baby. I'm happy for you. I can tell you're extremely excited, because you didn't even take a breath, telling me all of that. I know I have been giving you a hard time about taking that job, but I really am proud of you. I know you're my son, but more importantly you're a great man. Maybe you'll find a temporary friend among those country women in back woods, Tennessee to cook you some meals."

Laughing at his mother's stereotypical comment about southern women, Christian countered, "You are so wrong for that, these women are not much different from the women in L.A. Things are just as modern here as they are there, minus the smog and congestion."

"Uh huh, I'll bet they are," Iris teased. "What are your plans for the day?"

"I'm going to unpack in a few minutes. After that, I need to take care of some business. Later this afternoon, the Joseph's are planning a barbecue, so I'll be going back to their house. Hopefully, it won't be too much longer before I can get some rest. My body will have to get adjusted to the time change. With this place being two hours ahead of L.A., I know I'll be a little groggy for a few days."

"I'm sure you'll be fine. Don't worry about anything here, I'll take care of things on this end. You focus your attention on that youth center so that you can get finished and come back home."

Christian completed the call with his mother and unpacked his belongings. Once he was settled into the apartment, he returned phone calls and checked in with his assistant. *This would be a good time to catch up on emails,* he thought.

Time seemed to have passed by quickly. The telephone

rang loudly, startling him and pulling his attention away from the computer. During his quick assessment of the apartment, he didn't notice the telephone sitting on the table next to the couch. He answered the phone with his usual greeting. "This is Christian."

"Hey Christian, this is Daniel. Did I catch you at a bad time?"

Upon hearing the familiar voice, he relaxed. "No, not at all, what's going on?"

"The food is just about ready. I was wondering if you would like for me to send someone to pick you up, or would you prefer to drive on over?"

Christian appreciated having an option. He treasured his independence and didn't like having to depend on anyone. "How about you give me the address and I'll drive myself. That way no one will have to leave on my account."

"No problem." Daniel recited the address to Christian. "Everything should be ready in about an hour. Your apartment is only about ten to fifteen minutes from us. Give me a call if you need anything, otherwise we'll see you in a little while."

Christian ended the call with Daniel, and finished unpacking. He then took a shower and got dressed in a pair of jeans, and a hunter green polo shirt. Black loafers completed his outfit. Checking the time, he slid his phone into his pocket, grabbed his keys and headed out the door.

❖ ❖ ❖ ❖

A cloud of smoke rose from the back of the house. Christian inhaled deeply. The aroma from the grill was intoxicating, his stomach grumbled in response. If the food tasted as good as it smelled, he knew he was in for a treat.

Several cars lined the driveway. Laughter reverberated from the back of the house.

Christian climbed the three steps that led to the front door and pressed the doorbell. Within what seemed like seconds, a short chubby bi-racial girl with a long, curly ponytail answered the door.

Looking at Christian oddly, she asked, "May I help you?"

He smiled at the little girl, "Hello, my name is Christian Tyler. Are your parents home?"

"Just a moment." The little girl turned and yelled into the other room. "Mom, there's a man named Christian at the door."

Deborah came to the door wiping her hands on a towel. She unlocked the screen door and pushed it open. "Come on in, Mr. Tyler. Everyone is out back. I'll show you to the patio. Placing her arm around her daughter's shoulder she turned to the little girl and said, "Lanay, honey, this is Mr. Tyler. This is the man from California who is going to build the youth center."

Extending her hand to Christian, Lanay looked at him with a smile that reflected in her eyes. "It's nice to meet you, Mr. Tyler."

With a smile of his own, Christian enclosed the young girls hand in his and accepted her handshake. "It's nice to meet you also, Lanay."

Christian followed Deborah to the back patio where Daniel, Landon, and numerous others were sitting around picnic tables. Daniel rose and made introductions.

"How was the drive over?" Daniel asked. "I'm sure it was different from driving in L.A."

"It was definitely different from L.A. I have been in

countless traffic jams, but I can honestly say this was the first one that was caused by a slow moving tractor."

Everyone laughed at Christian's response. Daniel and his friends engaged him in conversation as they ate.

He met several board members and each of the children Daniel and Deborah had adopted. They made every effort to make sure Christian was comfortable, and that he felt welcome. Briefly, he discussed plans for the youth center, and confirmed the time they would meet the following morning.

"Landon told me you could throw down, Daniel, but he didn't do you any justice. Man, these ribs are so good I almost bit my finger. Everything is absolutely delicious. I'm so full, I feel like I'm going to burst." Christian patted his stomach to emphasize his statement.

Daniel patted himself on the back. "Why thank you, Christian. I try, I try."

"Oh, please don't swell this man's head up any bigger than it already is. If it gets any bigger, he won't fit in the house," Deborah teased.

Christian continued his visit for a couple of hours before excusing himself and returning to his apartment.

Once he was back inside of the apartment, Christian took another shower and dressed for bed. He laid out the blueprints for the youth center, and examined its contents.

With each passing minute, his eyes grew heavier, and heavier.

He was grateful for the kindness that was shown towards him in Bethany. He still was uncertain why he had been so adamant about taking on the task that lied ahead of him, but he believed in his heart that everything happened for a reason. Bethany Tennessee was only one piece of the puzzle. Christian was determined to keep an opened mind, as he focused on the bigger picture. Philanthropy had always been one of his desires. Building the youth center would afford him the opportunity to achieve that dream in a big way.

Following a big stretch, he slid between the sheets of the soft bed and nestled his head on the pillow. He was overcome with exhaustion. Instead of surrendering to the sleep his body desperately needed, he laid there making mental notes. Starting a new project always seemed to leave him restless.

Chapter Three

Thanks to the navigation system, Christian drove directly to the construction site where a mobile office had been set up. Surveying the site, he visualized the center. Prior to his arrival in Bethany, the architect sent him spec sheets and sketches of the proposed building.

Although Christian had made a career as a building contractor, he felt like there was something more for him in Bethany than simply doing a job. In his heart, Christian knew eventually he would find his true purpose for being there.

Daniel arrived at the site shortly after Christian. He took him inside and formally introduced him to the board of directors. Christian presented his plan to the board and listened to their recommendations. They spent the majority of the day discussing everything from the building materials, to sub-contractors, and timelines. Christian was inundated with meeting after meeting.

By the time they decided to call it quits for the day he was exhausted and hungry. The board offered to take him to dinner, an invitation to which he quickly accepted. Being new in town, he wanted to take advantage of every opportunity to familiarize himself with his temporary surroundings.

Christian followed close behind as Daniel and the other board members pulled into Sunset Restaurant and

Grill. The layout of the restaurant impressed him. One area of the restaurant catered to the casual diner. It was designed much like most sports bars, with large flat-screen televisions on every wall tuned to ESPN. Wooden tables with metal napkin holders, salt and pepper shakers, and bottles of ketchup, were surrounded by padded chairs. Various video games stood in the corner. A wall separated one area of the dining room from the other. The wait staff were dressed in screen printed t-shirts with the restaurant's logo on it, giving the eatery a more casual feel.

On the other side, the tables were dressed with ivory tablecloths, floating candles, and cloth napkins held together with silver rings. Unlike the casual side, the staff on the semi-formal side was adorned in white shirts and black pants. Within minutes, the hostess escorted them to their table.

Seated, Christian carefully examined the menu. The extensive selection contained meals varying from hamburgers to prime rib. "This is neat. I've never seen a restaurant like this before."

Daniel smiled. "I agree. This restaurant has been here for a couple of years now, and they seem to be doing very well. We don't have a lot of restaurants to choose from here in Bethany, so this works out pretty good. It's a good place to dine, whether you are in a group or alone. It's also a nice place to bring a date."

"Where'd that come from?" Christian asked while looking at Daniel with a sidelong glance.

Chuckling, Daniel patted Christian on the back. "Nowhere man, I'm just talking. Don't pay me any attention. Look, here comes the waitress to take our orders."

The soft buzz of conversation throughout the dining

room was interrupted by the boisterous laughter of a woman sitting across the room.

Christian shifted his gaze, and focused on the woman and her much older male companion. Based on her body language Christian supposed the couple was on a date. He tried to not stare at them but the woman held his gaze. She toyed with her long wavy tresses with her fingers and gently caressed the gentleman's wrinkled hand with her other hand. Her smooth caramel colored skin appeared pampered. The short skirt she was wearing revealed long toned legs. He couldn't explain it, but Christian felt drawn to the woman.

Thaddeus, one of the board members noticed Christian staring at the woman. "Man, you don't want to go there. She's a straight up gold digger."

He took one last look at her, noting Thad's words of warning.

The waitress returned with their meals, pulling Christian's attention back to his table.

The tantalizing aroma from the pecan encrusted salmon and wild rice medley he ordered made his mouth water. Bowing his head briefly, he said grace over his meal before peeling off a piece of salmon.

Christian poured himself into the conversation with the board members to keep his attention off the woman and her companion. Relief swept over him when he saw them rise to leave. Shortly thereafter, Daniel signaled to the waitress for the check.

An exhausted Christian arrived back at his apartment, worn out from the day's events. He went straight to the bedroom where he undressed quickly, and allowed the hot pulsating water from the shower to massage his aching muscles. Standing directly under the showerhead, he tried to wash away thoughts of the woman in the restaurant. It had been a long time since a woman held his attention so intently.

"This is crazy," he confessed aloud. "I don't even know that woman. For all I know, that could have been her husband she was with."

Frustrated, he got out of the shower, dried his body, and slipped into a pair of pajamas.

Christian went to bed. Although his normal routine included reading emails, and checking his social media accounts, he chose to omit it. At the moment, sleep was the only thing that held his interest. Pulling the covers up to his waist, Christian placed his hands behind his head and stared at the ceiling.

Sleep eluded him.

"Man, what's up with this?" Christian yelled, pounding his fist on the bed. Pushing the covers back forcefully, he got out of the bed and went into the living room. *I'm obviously not going to get any sleep tonight.*

He grabbed the remote control off the coffee table, sat down on the couch, and scanned the channels. Finally settling on ESPN, he watched Sports Center until he was overcome by sleep.

Chapter Four

Sunlight beamed through the sheer curtains announcing the morning. Christian waved his hands in an effort to shield his eyes from the bright light. The smell of fresh coffee from the pre-set automatic coffee maker awakened his senses.

Standing, he stretched his arms out. A dull ache in his side reminded him that he had spent the night on the sofa, and not in the comforts of the bed.

Massaging his side, he walked into the bathroom and prepared to start his day.

Christian dressed before checking the day's schedule on his tablet. He was glad to see that he only had a few tasks to complete. Although he was trying hard to get adjusted to the time zone change, he still suffered from a bit of jetlag. He found himself growing tired when he should have been wide awake.

He moved into the kitchen and poured a hot cup of coffee. Next, he placed a couple slices of bread into the toaster, which he covered in butter after they popped up. He grabbed an apple and headed into the dining room.

Settling down he nibbled on his breakfast and opened his laptop to prepare for work. Chewing a bite of toast, he washed it down with a sip of coffee. He worked tirelessly for several hours.

The cell phone rang, providing Christian with a much

needed distraction. Looking at the display he smiled at the familiar number on the screen. Making his way into the living room, he plopped down on the sofa, and placed his feet on the coffee table.

"What up, Blake," he yelled enthusiastically.

"Not a thing, man. What's up with you? Have they got you wearing overalls and a straw hat yet?" Blake laughed. "I'll bet you just finished watching Hee Haw."

"Dude, you are ignorant." Christian laughed along with Blake. "It's actually pretty decent here. The people seem to be nice, which is way different from L.A. I'm not going to lie, when I first got here I was trippin'. I was driving down the street and people were waving. Look, dawg, not just people on the street, but people passing in cars and stuff too. I felt kind of stupid when I told Daniel about what happened. I asked him how many people they told about me being here. Man, he just busted out laughing and,"

"Man, you been driving down there?" Blake asked cutting him off mid-sentence. "Did you rent a car or something?"

"No, actually, they gave me a car to use while I'm here. But, check this out, there is one thing I cannot get used to."

"What's that?"

"Getting stuck in traffic behind tractors and big farm machines. Dude, they drive down the main street like they are cars or something. When I first saw it, it tripped me out."

Blake and Christian both exploded with laughter. "I'll bet it's driving you up a wall being there. I mean going from L.A., where everything is super fast paced, to driving behind tractors. It's gotta feel like being in another world."

"It's definitely different, that's for sure," Christian agreed.

Changing the direction of the conversation, Blake asked, "Have you been trying to get with any of those country girls? I'll bet all of them have those cornbread booties."

Christian doubled over with laughter. "Man, you are stupid. What exactly is a cornbread booty? As a matter of fact, forget I asked you that. That's not even what I'm here for. My job keeps me pretty busy. Besides, what am I going to do with a woman this far away from home?"

"Do you really want me to answer that question?" Blake asked in a serious tone.

Christian couldn't help but to laugh at his best friend. "I said what would I do with one, not what would you do, because half of L.A. knows the answer to that."

"I guess you've got a point," Blake conceded. "You're not missing anything on this end. Everything is about the same as it was before you left. I went by to check on your mom to see if she needed anything, but she said she was okay."

"I appreciate you going by to check on mom. Make sure you keep me posted on everything on that end."

"For sure, man. I got you. But for real, dawg, you better listen to me. Check out those country chicks. I always heard they were good, you feel me."

"Yeah, all right man, I hear you." Thankful to hear everyone was doing well, Christian concluded his conversation with Blake. As much as he enjoyed talking to Blake, he knew that if he didn't end the call soon Blake would continue talking for another hour. "Listen man, I better get back to work."

"I understand, we'll talk soon," Blake replied.

Christian pressed the End button on his cell phone and

checked the clock. He had a few hours to go before his meeting so he decided to go to the grocery store.

Following the route, he normally took to the worksite, he pulled into the shopping center and found an empty parking space.

Once he was inside the store he located the produce section. Christian carefully selected fresh fruit and vegetables that would last a while without spoiling. Having been on his own since graduating college at the age of 21, Christian had settled into bachelorhood well. With an unpredictable travel schedule, he had also learned how to easily adjust to new environments.

After gathering his produce, he headed to the deli. His throat immediately felt dry when he looked up and saw the woman from the restaurant standing near the counter. *She's even beautiful in jeans and a t-shirt.*

❀ ❀ ❀ ❀

Shelby examined the selection of deli meats and cheeses and gave her order to the clerk. She normally dined out several times a week so she bought food that was quick and easy to prepare. Turning to place the packages in her shopping cart, she noticed Christian standing nearby. Feeling certain that he had been eyeing her, she smiled at him and said hello.

Caught completely off guard, Christian found his voice and uttered, "Hi."

Shelby smiled and walked away. She was used to the attention she received from men. Since the age of eighteen, she had gone out of her way to make sure she was attractive. Her Indian and Black heritage gave her smooth, caramel brown skin, a slender frame, and long black naturally wavy hair. Her wardrobe consisted of form fitting clothes and an assortment of high heeled shoes. When she dressed casually her jeans were always tight, and her t-shirts were V-neck.

❀ ❀ ❀ ❀

"Sir, is there something I can help you with?"

Christian turned and looked at the deli clerk. The irritation on her face embarrassed him. Staring at Shelby as she walked away had caused him to hold up the line. "I'm sorry, I'd like a half pound of smoked turkey and a half pound of honey ham cut in thin slices, please."

Christian received his deli order and continued his shopping. He headed to the snack aisle in search of potato chips. Focused on the task at hand, he didn't pay any attention to his surroundings.

"Are you following me now?"

Christian looked up only to find the woman standing a few feet away from him. "No, I'm not following you." He replied sarcastically.

"My, aren't we testy. I was just trying to make conversation." She crossed her arms and stared at Christian waiting for a response. The smell of his cologne was intoxicating. After a few seconds of awkward silence, she extended her hand to him. "I'm Shelby, and you are?" Subtly scanning his muscular chestnut brown frame, she smiled with intense delight.

Accepting her hand, Christian shook it and replied, "I'm Christian, nice to meet you, Shelby."

The firm grip of his hand sent a warm sensation throughout her body. She couldn't help but notice the three thousand dollar Gucci watch he was wearing. "Christian, huh? That's an interesting name. You're not from around here, are you? I can tell by your accent."

"No, I'm not. I'm from Los Angeles."

"Oh, okay. You're pretty far from home. What brings you all the way to Bethany? It's not exactly a big city. In fact, it's just a hole in the wall, if you ask me."

With caution, Christian continued his conversation with Shelby. He couldn't help but to recall Thad's words of caution at the restaurant. "I'm here on business," he responded flatly. Christian's phone rang giving him the excuse he needed to end his conversation with Shelby. "Excuse me, I need to take this."

"I understand. It was nice meeting you, Christian. Maybe I'll see you around sometimes."

"All right. It was nice meeting you as well," he said stepping away from Shelby.

He pushed the button to answer the call. "This is Christian. Hold on for just a second." Keeping the caller waiting, Christian pushed his shopping cart to the self checkout to complete his purchase. Feeling overwhelmed he decided to end his call. "Let me call you back in a minute, I'm tied up at the moment."

Christian gathered his bags and hurried to the car. Tossing the bags in the trunk, He maneuvered his way through the parking lot and returned to his apartment.

Quickly putting the groceries away, Christian pulled out his phone and returned the call to his office manager. Following a few rings, Shantrice answered with excitement. "What's going on?" Christian asked, acknowledging her enthusiasm.

"Well, Sir, I received a letter from Rising Star Studios. They have accepted our bid for their new 200,000 square foot studio. The best part is the projected start date is twelve months out, so it won't conflict with the youth center project."

Christian was elated. Things were working out in his favor. "That's excellent news, Shantrice. Can you imagine how many people we will be able to employ?"

"I know, Sir. I couldn't wait for our weekly call, I had to tell you about this today."

Shantrice began working for Christian ten years prior, as a receptionist, when he started his first construction company. Realizing his company was a startup, she'd agreed to work for minimum wage. With the growth of the company, Christian rewarded her dedication with steady promotions. Shantrice was the only person he trusted enough to leave in charge of his company while he was away.

"This is a brilliant example of when you do good to others, good things come back to you." Rethinking his statement, Christian declared "I don't mean that in an arrogant way. I didn't come here with the expectation of getting anything in return."

"Christian," Shantrice called out gaining his attention. "You don't have to explain. I know what you mean. This is a great blessing. It's okay for you to be happy." Laughing she continued, "You are too much for me. Sometimes you're too modest for your own good. Enjoy this moment. We'll speak again soon."

"Sounds like a plan. Call me if you need anything." Christian ended the call and threw punches in the air, today was a good day indeed.

Chapter Five

Shelby watched as Christian drove out of the parking lot. She couldn't deny his apparent discomfort when she spoke with him. That didn't deter her at all. She was determined to find out more about him. Shelby wondered what line of business he was in that would bring him from Los Angeles to Bethany.

Although she was having dinner with another man, she noticed him dining with several of Bethany's prominent businessmen at Sunset Restaurant. She had also noticed Thaddeus Bierman lean over and whisper something to him. She could only imagine what kind of venom he had spewed in Christian's ear about her. He'd hated her from the moment she and two of her co-workers filed sexual harassment claims against him while working at his family's hotel. His father chose to settle the cases out of court in order to keep his business and his family's name intact.

Pushing thoughts of Thaddeus from her mind, Shelby shifted her focus back to the handsome stranger that she only knew as Christian. One thing was for sure, if anybody could find out who he was her friend Dominique could do it. It was about time she gave Dominique a call.

Shelby arrived home and put her groceries away. After preparing a light snack, she carried it into the living room and sat in front of the television. Adjusting herself, she pulled her feet up, tucking them between the cushions of the couch. She picked up the remote and pressed the On

Demand button to select her favorite sitcom. Since her evenings were frequently occupied she made it a point to record the shows she didn't want to miss. Several episodes later Shelby's eyes grew heavy. As if on cue, she drifted off to sleep.

A loud bang on the door abruptly ended her nap. She jumped up from the couch, and knocked a cup of water onto the floor. "Who is it?" she yelled. Stomping to the door she looked through the peep hole to preview her obnoxious guest.

Her friend, Kim stood on the other side of the door smiling. "Just open the door, chick. I'm tired of standing out here looking crazy."

Shelby pulled hard on the door, causing it to bang against the wall. "What's wrong with you, banging on my door like you have lost your mind?"

Pushing her aside, Kim ignored Shelby's question and walked into the townhouse stopping in the kitchen.

"I'm hungry, what you got in here to eat?" Kim continued to go through the refrigerator and cabinets until she had the fixings for a turkey and cheese sandwich. She placed a handful of potato chips on her plate and poured herself a glass of fruit juice.

Shelby folded her arms across her chest and leaned against the wall. "Just make yourself at home, why don't you." She urged sarcastically. "I mean, don't mind me. I just live here and pay all the bills that's all."

"Girl please, you and I both know you ain't paying no bills up in here. You haven't paid your own bills in years." Kim bit back. Gathering her plate and glass, Kim headed into the living room and took a seat on the couch in front of the television.

"Are you going to tell me what you're doing here unannounced, or am I going to have to guess. I was sleeping good before you started banging on that doggone door too."

Kim took a bite of her sandwich and washed it down with juice. "Girl, I just came to see what you were up to. I was at home bored as I don't know what, so I figured I would come over here and hear your latest gossip. You know I live vicariously through you." Kim turned to face Shelby on the couch. "So tell me, what's been going on?"

Shelby eyed her friend suspiciously. "Wait a minute, let me get this straight. So you mean to tell me, you left your house where you have a husband, children, a dog, and a kitchen of your own to come over here, and eat up my food? Plus, on top of all of that, you expect me to entertain you with my business?"

"Exactly." Kim replied nodding her head and smiling. "Now, give up the goods."

"You are a mess." Shelby shook her head and laughed at her friend. "Hold up a minute."

Shelby went to the linen closet and grabbed a towel to soak up the water she spilled on the carpet. "I haven't been up to very much. Pretty much the same ole stuff. I'm still seeing William casually. He's taking care of business like he's supposed to, but I'm getting bored. It's about time to drop him."

Nodding her head as if she was agreeing with someone, Shelby blurted out, "Ooh wee, Kim girl, I saw this cutie today at the grocery store. He's a little shorter than what I'm used to, but I can adjust, I'll just have to wear my three inch heels instead of my six inch heels. He's not from here either. He's from Los Angeles. He told me he was here on business. His phone interrupted us before I got any more details."

"You are a trip, Shelby. You change men with the seasons. I don't know how you keep them all straight. I can barely keep up with my one man. You on the other hand juggle men like bowling pins. I don't see how you have the energy."

"Whatever, girl you can think what you want to think. Don't get it twisted. Men are supposed to take care of us, not the other way around. If a man thinks I'm going to take care of him he can kiss my rhythm because baby girl, I ain't the one. Don't hate the player, hate the game, baby. Besides, men do it all the time. It's not like I'm sleeping with all these men. In case you didn't know, I love me better than that. Nobody is getting my goodies, I'm all tease. I'm just exercising my survival skills."

Pursing her lips, Kim rolled her eyes at Shelby. "Survival skills huh? Do your thing then, girl, I ain't mad at you. Just be careful because folks are crazy these days."

Kim rose and went to the kitchen. She washed her dishes and returned them to the cabinet. With over twenty years of friendship to her credit, she had no problem making herself at home when she came to Shelby's house. Within minutes she returned to the living room and plopped down on the couch next to Shelby.

"So what's up with this dude, Christian? I wonder if his name is indicative of his lifestyle. In other words, I wonder if he is a Christian, because you sure are not."

"Forget you, Kim." Shelby pushed her almost knocking her off the couch. Their laughter echoed off the walls. Shelby and Kim continued to chat for several minutes before Kim's husband called summoning her home.

Chapter Six

Like clockwork Shelby arrived at the fitness center at 6:30 am. For her, maintaining a curvy size eight figure was not optional, it was absolutely mandatory. She stretched for several minutes before taking her place on the elliptical machine. Plugging in her headphones, she placed a bottle of water in the holder and began her workout. The exclusive gym had small televisions made into each treadmill, elliptical machine, and stationary bike. For Shelby, the one hundred dollar a month membership fee was worth every penny. In addition to the standard exercise equipment, the state of the art gym offered its clientele personal training, aerobic exercises, an Olympic sized heated swimming pool, hot tubs, saunas, and spa treatments.

Lying on the massage table following her workout, Shelby went over her mental to do list for the day. It was time for her to update her wardrobe, which meant a trip to Memphis. The soothing music and skillful hands of the masseur relaxed each of her tense muscles until she found herself falling asleep. Forty-five minutes later she was up and preparing for the day.

The clock inside her new Pacific Sky Blue Infiniti Q60 displayed 8:30am. Shelby keyed the number for City Hall into her cell phone. The automated system picked up after two rings. She entered Dominique's extension and waited for her friend to answer.

Dominique answered the phone with her usual greeting, "Good Morning, Mayor's office, Dominique speaking how may I assist you?"

"How many times a day do you have to say that? You and I both know you are not that perky in the morning," Shelby teased.

Taking on a completely different tone, Dominique laughed and replied, "I know that's right girl, but it's my job and you know I gots to pay the bills. What's up, Shelby?"

"Not too much, I need a little bit of help with something, and I figured you were the perfect person to contact. I mean with you being the Mayor's personal assistant and all, I know you have access to certain info."

"I should have known you were up to something," Dominique teased. "What you got?"

"Have you heard of a man by the name of Christian who is here from Los Angeles on business? I'm not sure of the last name."

"It's funny you should ask me that. Hold on just a second." Dominique laid the phone down on her desk, Shelby could hear a file cabinet close in the background followed by the sound of papers being shuffled. Dominique returned to the line, "Here it is. There is a contractor here working on a project for the new youth center that is being built called A Mother's Love. His name is Christian Tyler." After giving Shelby the requested information, Dominique expressed her curiosity. "Why do you need to know about this guy?"

Shelby tried to think of a realistic reason to give Dominique, but she knew her friend would read through anything other than the truth. "I met him the other day in the grocery store. He gave me his first name, but he had to leave before I got any more information. You know me, when I want to know something, it will haunt me until I find out. I can't stand being in the dark about stuff."

"That's true, you've been that way for as long as I have known you. You better be careful, girl. You know what they say, curiosity killed the cat."

"Yeah, I know." Shelby hurried off the phone before Dominique could ask any more questions. "Ooh, girl, look at the time, I better let you get back to work."

Dominique was her girl, but she was also very nosy. Shelby couldn't allow her any more access into her plans than she already had. Armed with a name and a line of business Shelby hurried home to do some research. Before any further pursuits she needed to know if Christian Tyler would be worth her time.

Tossing her gym bag into the laundry room, Shelby went into the kitchen and fixed herself a light breakfast. She sat at the table and devoured her food before turning her attention to her tablet.

Tapping on the Internet browser, she keyed Christian Tyler, Los Angeles, California into the search engine. With sheer delight, she shrieked when she saw all of the results that popped up including a link to his company in L.A. Hurriedly, she tapped on the website's photo gallery and viewed several luxury homes and businesses that had been built by his company.

After viewing the website, she went back to the search engine and viewed some of the other information about Christian.

An hour later Shelby felt like she knew him personally. She had reviewed everything from his business dealings, to his friends in each of the online social networks he was affiliated with. Based on the information she gathered, she believed Christian was single and he didn't have any children.

Armed with a wealth of information, she was ready to begin her pursuit. Christian Tyler had better be ready, because what Shelby wants, Shelby gets.

Chapter Seven

Christian studied the blueprints for the center. He was pleased with the architect's thoroughness. A couple weeks of perfect weather allowed the foundation to be laid and solidified. Construction of the center was underway. Feeling a twinge of homesickness, Christian worked fourteen to sixteen hour days to occupy his time. Although he was in constant contact with his mother and close friends, it wasn't the same as being at home. One thing was for sure, small town life was not for him. He missed the hustle and bustle of Los Angeles.

He couldn't believe he had been in Bethany six weeks. Time was passing by quickly. There were a few things he enjoyed and was sure he would miss upon returning home. The air in Bethany was extraordinarily clear, refreshing him with every breath he took. He would also miss the clear, star filled sky. Something about the small town was euphoric. Most of the people he came in contact with were friendly. He had finally gotten used to strangers waving at him as he drove down the street. He even waved back most of the time.

After tying up loose ends at the office, Christian decided to head to the Sunset Restaurant and Grill for dinner. He had become a frequent diner since his initial meal with the board of directors. Some of the servers had become familiar enough with him that they greeted him by name. Personally, he preferred the casual side of the restaurant. As usual he took a seat in front of one of the large televisions. The Memphis Grizzlies were in a heated third quarter battle against the   Los Angeles Lakers. He was pleased to see his team was holding its ground.

Shortly after he sat down, a tall, full figured, young woman with a mocha complexion and naturally curly hair came to take his order. "How are you today, Christian?"

"I'm doing well, Laneise. How are you?"

"Couldn't be better," she replied. "What can I get for you today?" Armed with pen and pad, Laneise stood ready to take his order.

"Give me the hot wings and onion blossoms. To drink, I'll have Coke."

"Sounds good, I'll be right back with your order."

"Thanks Laneise."

Ten minutes later, Laneise returned with Christian's meal. Smoke rose from the chicken revealing its heat. Christian slowly devoured the entire meal. With his eyes glued to the television he didn't notice Shelby come into the restaurant.

Shelby saw Christian sitting in front of the television and felt a wicked smile form on her lips. *This couldn't have been better, if I had planned it myself,* she thought.

From the bar, she had a clear view of Christian's table. She could tell he was finished with his meal and therefore would probably be leaving soon. In order to leave the restaurant, he would have to pass by the bar where he would find her sitting.

The final buzzer rang, and the Lakers celebrated another victory. Christian placed the cost of his meal and tip inside the small black folder Laneise left on the table for him.

Rising from the table, he stretched lightly before heading towards the door. As soon as he turned he noticed Shelby sitting at the bar. He was pleasantly surprised to find her sitting alone, but he didn't dare jump to any conclusions. For all he knew she could have been waiting on her boyfriend to join her.

At the risk of embarrassing himself, Christian determined he wouldn't speak to her unless she spoke first. What was he thinking? She probably didn't even remember him. Moving quickly, he walked in the direction of the bar.

With calculated precision, Shelby turned and faced Christian head on. Seductively, she smiled and greeted him in a low tone. "Hello, Christian."

Christian stopped a few feet away from her. He was surprised she had remembered his name. He blew off her greeting as Southern Hospitality. Not wanting to appear rude, Christian returned the smile. "Hello, Ms…"

"Shelby. Shelby Lamar."

"Please forgive me, Ms. Lamar." Christian bowed his head in the position of a Chinese greeting.

Shelby continued flirting. "So we meet again, what a coincidence."

"Are you sure you're not following me, Shelby?" Christian teased.

"Of course not," she replied. "I'm here picking up my dinner. In case you haven't noticed they offer carry out as well."

"I was just messing with you. Enjoy your dinner."

Before Shelby could continue the conversation any further Christian was out the door. "Why is he running away from me!"

Once Christian walked out a waitress brought Shelby a plastic bag containing her meal. She quickly paid and rushed out of the door hoping to catch Christian in the parking lot before he left. Shelby exhaled when she saw Christian outside talking to one of the men he had been dining with when she first saw him. She smirked when she saw she still had a chance to gain his attention. Realizing she needed a plan, she dropped her keys on the seat through the slightly opened window. If he was the man she hoped he was, Christian would be gentleman enough to help her retrieve her keys. She wasn't worried about her plan backfiring because she always kept a spare key tucked inside her wallet.

Christian noticed Shelby peering inside a car parked in front of him. "Did you lose something?" he asked approaching her.

She looked up in mock surprise. "Oh, hi again. It seems I've locked my keys in my car. They must have fallen out of my purse as I was getting out. I can't believe I was so careless. I have no idea what I'm going to do now."

Assessing the slightly opened window, Christian soon realized it was impossible to get the keys without assistance. It was times like this that he was glad he opted to pay the small monthly fee on his cell phone for roadside assistance.

Turning to Shelby, Christian spoke with concern, "There is no way I can get the keys out of your car. However, I can call roadside assistance and have them to come and open the door for you."

"I'd hate to inconvenience you like that. Let me see if I can get one of my friends to come and pick me up, I believe I have a spare key at home." Shelby pulled out her cell phone and pretended to make a few calls. Exhaling roughly, she turned to Christian. "I can't get anybody."

"Really, it's no problem, let me call roadside assistance and get you some help." Christian pulled out his phone and dialed the number for assistance.

Within seconds a dispatcher was on the line. He recited the car details and location information. Following a brief hold, the dispatcher returned to the line and informed him that the locksmith was in route and should be there within 15 minutes.

Christian shared the information he received from the dispatcher with Shelby and gave her the option to return inside the restaurant to wait or to sit inside his car.

In an effort to downplay her forwardness Shelby opted to sit inside the restaurant, using her uneaten meal as an excuse. Christian volunteered to stay outside, and wait for the locksmith. Twenty minutes later the locksmith arrived and unlocked Shelby's car door.

Shelby accepted the keys from Christian and gave him a hug. "Thank you so much."

"No problem. Have a good night." He walked past Shelby and climbed into his car. His heart was racing. He didn't know what it was about that woman, but Shelby Lamar made him nervous. She brought up feelings in him he'd almost forgotten he had. Turning the key in the ignition, Christian noticed Shelby trying to get his attention. He rolled down the window in response.

"Christian, I just want to tell you again how thankful I am to you for helping me. I really appreciate it."

"You're welcome, I'm glad I was able to help."

"Tell you what, why don't I give you my number and the next time you're dining alone you can give me a call. I may be able to join you."

Hesitating, Christian smiled and replied, "That's kind of you." He turned and searched for a pen.

Making sure Christian wouldn't have an excuse not to take her phone number, Shelby pulled out her cell phone and interrupted his search. "Don't bother looking for a pen. I'll just call you now from my phone and when my number comes up you can save it in your phone.

Christian eyed her suspiciously. He wasn't sure giving Shelby his phone number was a wise decision, but the thought of having a dinner companion other than his business associates was appealing. He called out his number to her and watched as she keyed the numbers into her phone. His phone rang notifying him of her call. "Got it," he said.

"Okay good. Don't be a stranger." Shelby turned quickly and got into her car. She had made her first move and thrown out the bait. Given a little time, she was sure she would reel him in.

❀ ❀ ❀ ❀

What just happened? Christian thought to himself. One minute he was watching the Lakers gain another victory, and the next minute he was exchanging phone numbers with a beautiful woman. Maybe he was being naïve, but he didn't see that coming at all. He turned into the apartment complex parking lot and hurried inside.

Sitting on the couch, he propped his feet up on the coffee table and tuned the television to his favorite sports channel.

Christian tried unsuccessfully to focus on the sports broadcaster. There was no doubt he was flattered by Shelby's advances, but he could not allow her to distract him from his job. On the other hand, he was intrigued by her. Although her beauty was obvious, there was something about her that appealed to him. He wanted to get to know her, but Thaddeus' warning kept him at bay.

Why am I wasting my time focusing on that woman? I came here to build a youth center, that's it. I don't have time for this, he scolded himself. Entering the bedroom, he changed into his pajamas and prepared for bed.

Maybe Shelby is a part of the reason that I'm in Bethany, he thought. Only time would tell. Climbing into bed, Christian laid staring at the ceiling with thoughts of Shelby dominating his mind.

Chapter Eight

A gentle breeze danced in the curtains allowing sunlight to peer through. The harmonious chirping of birds outside her window woke Shelby up. There was no comparison to the smell of freshly cut grass mingled with flowers. She felt refreshed. The dawning of a new day, especially when the sun was shining gave her a sense of peace. She viewed each new day as a new beginning. It was her way of coping with the lifestyle she lived. Her life had taken an unexpected turn which caused her to make decisions she wasn't proud of. The thought of giving up on her dreams depressed her. It seemed as though one minute she was heading in the direction she had dreamed of since childhood. The next minute she was forced to give up the thing she wanted most to step into a role she never asked for. She refused to focus on her past. In her opinion, looking back was pointless.

Sitting up on the bed, Shelby stretched her arms out and took a deep breath. She allowed her feet to dangle freely. Her mind drifted easily to Christian. There was something special about him. She couldn't put her finger on it but he seemed to be different from the other men she had dealt with in the past. The kindness he showed her, without seeking anything in returned confused her. She was used to men being open about what they expected from her in exchange for the financial support she received from them. She would have to take a different approach with Christian if she was going to make him hers. It was time she and Christian got better acquainted.

Grabbing her cell phone from the dresser, Shelby scrolled through her recent calls and retrieved Christian's number. She made it a point to save his number to her contacts list. Without hesitation, she pressed the Send button and waited for him to pick up.

"Hello," Christian answered in a deep groggy voice.

"Good morning, Christian, this is Shelby. Did I wake you?"

"That's okay, it's about time for me to get up anyway." Christian groaned slightly as he stretched. He sat up on the side of his bed. "I can't seem to get adjusted to the time difference between here and home. What's going on?"

"Not much. When I got up this morning I saw it was such a nice day, so I thought about you. I was wandering what a man this far away from home does on a Saturday. I couldn't think of anything, so I decided to call and ask you."

"Actually, not very much." Christian replied somberly. He had to admit, Shelby could keep his attention. He had to constantly remind himself that she was not the reason he was in Bethany. At the same time, he was beginning to get bored with the small town. "There doesn't seem to be much to do here."

"You're right. There isn't much to do here. In fact, I was thinking about going to Memphis today. Would you care to join me?" Shelby sat in quiet anticipation hoping he would agree.

Christian considered her offer. He didn't want to make it

a habit of spending time with Shelby, but he also didn't want to spend any more time in his apartment than necessary.

"That sounds like a good idea. I was hoping I would get to check out Memphis while I was here. What time are you planning on leaving?"

Shelby tried to mask the excitement in her voice. "I would like to leave in about an hour, is that enough time for you?"

"Yeah, that's plenty of time." Christian responded, standing to his feet.

"Where are you staying while you're in Bethany?" Shelby asked.

"I'm in the Bethany Terrace apartments. Building two apartment eight."

"Okay. Since I'm more familiar with this area than you are I'll drive, that is if you don't mind. I can call you when I'm on my way."

"Sounds like a plan." Christian ended his call with Shelby and headed into the bathroom to get ready.

Shelby leaped off the bed and examined the clothes in her closet. She had to be smart in her selection. Christian seemed to be a bit conservative so anything seductive would more than likely turn him off. Fashion was the thing she was most passionate about. Considering what they would do once they got to Memphis, Shelby opted for a soft pink fitted v neck t-shirt and white shorts. She chose white sandals to show off her pedicured feet. Finally, she decided to pull her hair up into a ponytail. She sprayed Juicy Couture Viva La Juicy cologne on her neck and wrist.

Darting out the door, she was excited about seeing Christian and having some alone time with him outside of Bethany. She figured the one-and-a-half-hour trip to

Memphis would give them the perfect opportunity to get to know each other.

❀ ❀ ❀ ❀

Shelby pulled into Bethany Terrace and located building two. Her breath caught in her throat when she saw Christian standing outside. He wore a white V-neck t-shirt that was tucked in the front. The short sleeves of the shirt, snugly fit his well toned arms. His muscles bulged slightly underneath. His jeans were a dark denim, accented with a black belt that had a large bronze buckle. He completed his outfit with white athletic shoes.

She pulled into an empty parking spot, unlocked the door, and waited for him to climb inside.

"Hey you," he greeted with a bright smile that displayed perfectly straight white teeth. The spicy musk of his cologne tickled her nose.

"Hey yourself," she replied matching his smile. "Are you ready to see the big city of Memphis? I'm sure it's miniscule in comparison to L.A."

"I am looking forward to it actually. I've heard some good things about Memphis. I know it may be cliché but I would like to get some barbecue while we're there."

Beaming with excitement, Shelby replied. "If barbecue is what you want, then we couldn't have picked a better time. The Memphis in May Barbecue Festival happens to be this weekend." Pointing at his feet, she warned "I hope those shoes are comfortable because we're going to do some serious walking today."

"It's all good," Christian replied.

Shelby backed out of the parking spot and steered her car in the direction of I-40 West. "I hope you like R&B

music," she stated before pushing the button to turn on the radio.

"As a matter of fact I do." Christian bobbed his head to the soulful sounds flowing through the car speakers."

Moving her shoulders in response to the music, Shelby nodded her head. "This is grown folk's music right here. What you know about that."

Christian angled his body so that he could observe Shelby. He enjoyed watching her move. "Oh, yeah. This is that old school. I know all about it. Music these days just isn't the same."

"I know that's right." Shelby accelerated and merged onto the interstate. Pushing the button on her steering wheel she lowered the volume on the radio. "So Christian, what brought you to Bethany? I wouldn't think someone from L.A. would have even heard of Bethany, let alone visit here."

"I saw a story about the youth center and I wanted to help. I figured I could use my skills as a building contractor to offer some assistance to the project."

Glancing at him briefly, Shelby furrowed her eyebrows. "You came all the way here from Los Angeles to help build a youth center?" Not wanting to come across as callus, she added, "I mean, I'm sure you must have multiple opportunities closer to home to do a project like that."

"Yes, L.A. does have numerous needs and opportunities. We also have more resources," he answered flatly.

"That makes sense," Shelby agreed. "I can remember when they were trying to get the money to build it. There were fundraisers everywhere. The stores and restaurants had fundraising jars on their counters. Several people sponsored car washes and bake sales. They even had children at the intersections with buckets to collect donations from drivers. Apparently it worked, I mean you're here."

Being in such close quarters with her, Christian had the opportunity to observe Shelby as she drove. He could no longer ignore how beautiful she was. Her smooth brown skin reminded him of a cup of hot chocolate. She had thick black lashes and perfectly arched eyebrows that enhanced her dark brown eyes. A slight gloss, glistened on her thick lips as she mouthed the words to Keith Sweat's song *Make It Last Forever*. She tapped her long, slender fingers on the steering wheel to the beat of the music. His gaze traveled downward. Her thighs were thick and toned. With her hair pulled up into a ponytail, Christian found himself desiring to kiss her neck.

Redirecting his attention, he stared out the window. He knew that if he didn't shift his focus quickly he wouldn't be able to mask his attraction much longer.

Christian relaxed against the back of the seat. "Now that you know about me, how about you tell me about you? Who is Shelby Lamar?"

The base in his voice pulsated in her ears. Adjusting herself in her seat, she let out a low moan. "Who is Shelby Lamar, huh?" she repeated. "I'm just Shelby, a woman that enjoys life. I work hard, and I play even harder."

Christian's demeanor changed immediately. He was trying his best to get to know Shelby, but Thaddeus' warning played in his ears. Refusing to ruin the moment, he delved deeper. "That's a pretty broad statement. Let me see if I can't narrow this down a bit," he chuckled. "Since you said you work hard and play even harder, what are you passionate about?"

Shelby's lips parted into a full grin. "That's easy. I love fashion. In fact, I've loved it for as long as I could remember. When I was little my mother bought me books full of paper dolls. I would grab my crayons and do all kinds of designs on the blank sheets. From paper dolls to constantly changing up my wardrobe, this interest has always been a part of my life in some form."

"Do you work in that industry now? No offence, but for someone to be as passionate as you seem to be, I would expect you to live in New York or Paris, not Bethany."

"Yeah, I know. Bethany isn't exactly the couture capital of the world. I currently work part-time at a boutique in Jackson that caters to women of all sizes. I'm also taking some classes online. After I get the basic coursework completed, I plan to move to a larger city where I can continue my studies and increase my skills." Shelby sighed in frustration. "I have wanted to get away from this place for as long as I can remember."

Christian was impressed with Shelby. He admired a woman with dreams and aspirations. The more he learned about her, the more he wanted to know. He couldn't deny his attraction to her. He watched as she easily maneuvered her car through the increased traffic. "You're handling this traffic like a pro. I wonder how well you'll do in L.A. traffic."

Shelby quickly turned her head in Christian's direction. "Where'd that come from?" she questioned.

Inwardly Christian squirmed. He didn't mean to verbalize his thoughts. Now he was in desperate need of a comeback to throw her off. "You said you wanted to move to a larger city to pursue your fashion career. So, I was simply comparing this traffic to the traffic in Los Angeles." He was hoping she bought the lame excuse that he himself didn't believe.

"Oh, okay," was Shelby's only response.

Exiting the highway, Shelby drove through downtown Memphis, pointing out things she thought Christian would be impressed with. "Over there is the Pyramid. It was the main sports venue before they built the Fed Ex Forum. Now it's a huge sporting goods store. And over there is the M bridge. At night they light it up, it's really pretty."

Pulling into a parking lot, Shelby smiled at Christian. "Let's go have some fun," she shrieked.

"Lead the way," he replied matching her enthusiasm as they exited the vehicle.

Following a brief walk, Shelby and Christian arrived at the riverfront. He inhaled deeply enjoying the delicious aroma coming from multiple grills and smokers. His stomach grumbled in response.

Shelby pointed to a green and white tent with Big Daddy's BBQ printed in bold letters on the side. "Ooh, you have to try their food. It's absolutely delicious." Taking him by the hand, she led him towards the tent.

The soft touch of her hand sent what felt like an electric current through Christian's body. It had been a long time since he'd been this close to a woman. After his last relationship ended, he chose to pour himself into his company.

"We'll both have the pulled pork and rib plate with plenty of sauce. For our side dishes, please give us mac and cheese and baked beans." Turning to Christian, she asked, "White bread or dinner roll?"

Extending his hand towards her, Christian smiled. "You choose."

"In that case, give us the roll. We'll have Arnold Palmers

to drink."

Christian stepped up to pay for their order. He grabbed the covered plates, utensils, and napkins off the table and led Shelby over to an empty picnic table.

Once they were seated Shelby reached into her small cross body purse and offered him hand sanitizer.

Bowing his head to say grace, Christian was immediately interrupted.

"Ah, hmm." Shelby pretended to clear her throat. Once she gained his attention she stated, "I was taught it's rude to exclude others when you say grace if you're dining together." Stretching her hand across the table, she reached for his hand.

"Oh, I apologize." Christian accepted her hand and uttered a quick prayer of thanks.

He picked up a rib and bit into the succulent smoked meat. "This is delicious," he declared.

Shelby placed a fork full of mac and cheese in her mouth. "Umm, yes it is," She agreed. "Big Daddy's is a local restaurant. I've eaten their food several times and I must say, they never disappoint." Taking a sip of the iced tea and lemonade mixture she joked, "Whenever I see their billboard on the highway I be like, hey Big Daddy."

Seeing Shelby with her eyes closed and her arm raised like she was in church, he couldn't help but laugh. "Wow, it's that good? In that case, I better take another bite."

Shelby joined him in laughter before indulging in another bite of food.

❀ ❀ ❀ ❀

Following their lunch, Shelby suggested they walk off their meals. They walked over to Beale Street and listened to a few live bands. They finally settled on B.B. King's

Blues Club. Christian enjoyed watching Shelby sway to the music.

Grabbing his hands, she pulled him onto the dance floor. Their bodies moved together in a rhythm of their own. Shelby turned and rested her back against Christian's chest. Instinctively he placed his arms around her waist holding her close. He inhaled the alluring scent of her hair. She placed her hands on top of his and allowed the music to take them on a euphoric journey.

Shelby inwardly wished this moment could go on forever. It had been so long since a man lovingly held her close. She felt safe in his arms. Unlike the other men that had been in and out of her life, she actually imagined a life with him.

Loud applause signaled the end of the song. Stepping away from Shelby was not an easy task. She'd felt so good in his arms. It felt as though she belonged there. Christian wanted to hold her, to outline her beautiful face with his fingers. He wanted to cover her mouth with his.

"Thank you for the dance." Once again Shelby had successfully pulled him away from his thoughts.

"The pleasure was all mine," Christian replied honestly. "We should probably take our seats." Placing his hand in the small of her back, he escorted her to their table.

"Would you like something to drink?" he asked once they were seated.

Fanning herself with a small drink menu on the table, Shelby was grateful for the offer. "Some sweet tea would be great. I'm thirsty."

Christian raised his hand to signal for the waitress. A young woman with short blonde hair bounced over to the table vigorously chewing gum.

"Hi, I'm Autumn. What can I get for y'all?"

"We'll have two glasses of iced tea please," Christian replied. "That'll be all."

The young waitress looked at him like he was from another planet. "Iced tea?" she questioned with a deep southern drawl. "Honey, do you want that sweet, unsweet, or Long Island."

Shelby watched the interaction between Christian and the waitress. She couldn't help but laugh. The expression on his face was priceless.

"Sweet, please," he stated firmly.

"Do you want some hot wings or anything with that tea?" she pressed, looking from Christian to Shelby.

"No, just the tea. That will be all."

"Humph," the waitress groaned. "I'll be right back with your tea."

Once the waitress walked away from the table, Shelby burst out in a full on laugh.

"So much for southern hospitality," Christian stated.

"Aww, you poor dear. She's probably having a bad day or something."

"Perhaps."

Christian and Shelby listened to the band play another set before leaving. They walked back to Shelby's car in virtual silence.

"So, Christian tell me, was Memphis all that you expected it to be?" Shelby asked as she pulled into the busy Memphis traffic.

"It was pretty cool. The food was good. I'm guessing Beale Street is its claim to fame."

"Yeah, I guess. Unless you're an Elvis fan," she replied.

"Ah, man, I forget Elvis was from Memphis. I gotta see

Graceland."

Shelby looked at Christian with a raised eyebrow. "Are you serious?" she asked.

Laughing, Christian replied, "No, I was only kidding. I have no interest in seeing Graceland."

Shelby matched his laughter. "Man, you had me going for a minute. To be honest, I think you were serious. You just tried to change your story when you saw my reaction. You know you're an Elvis fan. You probably have a pair of blue suede shoes in your closet in Cali. I'll bet those bad boys are wrapped in plastic, sitting on the shelf."

"How'd you guess?"

Christian and Shelby both erupted in laughter. Shelby turned on the radio and pretended to search for Elvis music. Placing his hand on top of hers, Christian pressed the button for the preprogrammed station Shelby had tuned into on their drive to Memphis.

"I'm sorry," he stated, realizing he still had his hand on top of hers. He pulled his hand back and cupped his hands together.

"It's okay," she replied. Confused by his sudden discomfort, Shelby placed both of her hands on the steering wheel. They spent the remainder of the trip riding silently listening to music.

A little over an hour later, Shelby pulled in front of Christian's apartment building and turned off the car's engine. "This has been an enjoyable day. I'm glad you decided to accompany me to Memphis. It was nice having some company."

"I had a great time as well. Thank you for inviting me. More than likely, I would have spent the entire day at this apartment catching up on work or something."

"I'll bet when you're home in L.A., you stay on the go. You don't seem like the type to sit at home all the time."

Christian considered her words. She couldn't be more wrong. With the exception of working, visiting his mother, or golfing with Blake, he spent most of his time at home.

"Believe it or not, I'm pretty much the same way when I'm at home," Christian responded. "The main difference is I have several business associates there, so I often have to attend various luncheons and dinner parties."

Shelby listened attentively. She wanted to get to know Christian better. He appeared to be quite reserved and she wondered why. They hadn't even parted ways yet and she was already looking forward to the next time she would get to see him.

The loud ring of Christian's cell phone broke the silence in the car. He pulled the phone from his pocket and checked the number. MOM displayed on the screen. Silencing the ringer, he turned to Shelby. "I guess I better take this before she sends out a search party."

Shelby smiled, "Believe me, I do understand. Besides I've kept you out all day. I need to head home anyway."

"We'll have to do this again sometime." Reaching over he placed his hand on top of hers and squeezed it gently.

"I'd like that," she replied.

His phone rang a second time. "I better go, be careful going home. Have a good night."

"Thanks, you too."

Christian exited the vehicle and answered the persistent ring.

Shelby thought of Christian and their day together on her drive home. Being with him gave her a sense of stability. She felt safe in his presence. For the first time, she felt like she had found a man that could give her genuine love. He was no longer someone to only take care of her financially. He was a man that she saw a future with. She just hoped he would eventually feel the same way.

Chapter Nine

"Where have you been? I've been sitting here over an hour waiting on you." Kim yelled as soon as Shelby turned the lock on the door.

"Excuse me, but what are you even doing here?" Shelby sat her purse down on the table. "As a matter of fact, how did you get in here?"

"Duh, I used the spare key that you leave in the flower pot outside." Kim replied as if Shelby should have already known the answer to her question.

Shelby crossed her arms and tapped her foot on the floor. "That key is for emergencies only. It's not for you to drop in whenever you feel like it. I keep telling you, you don't live here. You have your own house."

"Girl, please. You ain't talking about nothing. Now get over here and tell me where you've been." Kim popped another potato chip in her mouth.

"You better be glad I'm in a great mood right now, Kim. Seriously, we're going to have to discuss your reasons for constantly abandoning your family and coming over here."

"Yeah, yeah, yeah. Stop stalling and spill it." Kim demanded waving her off.

"I went to Memphis today," Shelby announced. "No big deal."

Eyeing her suspiciously Kim probed. "Who is he?"

Shelby laughed nervously. "How do you know it was a he? You act like you know everything about me, Kim." Rolling her eyes, she continued. "You get on my nerves."

Kim placed a hand on her ample hip. "Who do you think you're fooling, Shelby? I have known you since you were a child. For one, you're not going all the way to Memphis by yourself. For two, if you were going shopping you would have called me to see if I wanted to go. Me and Dominique are your only girlfriends, and I know she didn't go with you because I talked to her not too long ago."

"Darn, girl. I've told you, you missed your calling. You should be somebody's detective or working for the FBI. You're too nosy to be a housewife." Pressing her fingers against her lip, Shelby blew Kim a kiss. "But I love you with your nosy self."

Kim pulled her feet up on the couch and waited hungrily to hear Shelby's latest story.

Shelby wouldn't admit it, but she was glad Kim had been there waiting on her. She was so excited, she felt like she would burst if she had to hold her story in for too long. "I went with Christian."

"Wait," Kim interrupted. "Are you talking about the guy you met at the grocery store? The one from Los Angeles?"

"Yes, girl. That's the one."

"Boy, you move fast," Kim teased, snapping her fingers in the air.

"Shut up, Kim. I'm not thinking about you." Adjusting herself on the couch, Shelby continued. She replayed the entire day for her friend. Starting with her phone call that morning and ending with her driving home wishing he was there with her.

Kim sat in silence listening attentively to her best friend.

She felt like she knew Shelby better than anyone. She had never seen Shelby get this excited over any man. She didn't know who this Christian guy was, but whoever he was he had to be something special.

"Well, are you going to say anything? Or, are you just gonna sit there with that blank look on your face?" Shelby asked.

Shaking her head, Kim smiled at her friend. "Girl, you've got it bad. All I'm going to say is be careful. I mean he's not from here. I don't want you to get hurt. Please use caution."

"Ugh, you always have something negative to say, Kim. You get on my nerves, for real." Shelby planted her feet on the floor and prepared to stand.

"No, don't get upset. I'm just telling you to take it slow. You really like this guy, I can tell. You know me, Shelby. I've got your back no matter what." Scooting closer to her friend, Kim placed her arm around Shelby's shoulder. "Go for it. Who knows, he just might be the one."

Laying her head on Kim's shoulder, Shelby replied, "Thanks, girl."

The friends continued their visit until Kim noticed Shelby dozing off. "It's obvious you're tired. I'm going home so that you can get some rest."

"Okay, girl," Shelby replied between yawns. "I'll call you tomorrow."

Kim reached out and embraced her friend. "I'll let myself out. Goodnight, Shell."

"Goodnight."

❊ ❊ ❊ ❊

Christian stood outside and watched as Shelby drove away. He answered his mother's call after several rings.

"Hello, Mother. How are you this evening?"

"I'm doing well, Son. What's going on with you? I've called you at least three times. I know you weren't in a meeting or anything because it's Saturday."

"No, I didn't have a meeting. I typically don't have meetings on Saturday. I went and checked out Memphis today. It was pretty cool. I ate barbecue and listened to some music at B.B. Kings club on Beale Street."

Iris could tell Christian was holding something back. She also knew that he would not volunteer any information. Since childhood he had always been a private person keeping his feelings seemingly under lock and key. Usually by the time he revealed things to her, he had already made a decision on whatever matter he was facing.

"That sounds like fun. Did you go with some of the people you've been working with?"

"No. Actually I went with a woman I met at the grocery store." Christian thought back to how cold he must has seemed to Shelby on that day. He was vague with his answers to her and he rushed away from her the first chance he got.

"I must have really missed a lot. I had no idea you were seeing someone there."

"I would hardly call it seeing someone. She called this morning and asked if I had any plans and since I didn't she asked if I wanted to join her on a trip to Memphis."

"Oh, I see." Iris replied sarcastically. She knew better than to press because if she did he would shut down completely. "How's the youth center coming along?"

"The project is going very well. In fact, we're ahead of schedule. So far I haven't run into many issues which is always a good thing. The people here are also very appreciative. That always helps."

Iris exhaled roughly into the phone. "That's great, son. I'm glad to know things are going so well for you."

Christian was bothered by his mother's expression, something about her tone didn't feel right to him. "What's going on with you, Mom? You seem a little down. Before you say there's nothing wrong, remember I know you well enough to know when something is going on with you."

"I miss you, baby. It's weird not seeing you and having you so far away. You haven't traveled for a job in quite a while. I'd gotten used to you being around and now you're not. It's going to take some getting used to on my part."

"I understand. I miss you too. It won't be much longer until I'm home. Like I said before the project is ahead of schedule."

Christian spent the remainder of the conversation with his mother telling her about things he had seen and discovered in Bethany. She informed him about the water shortage in Los Angeles and other current events. At times they talked like mother and son, and other times they talked like old friends. Christian was grateful for the relationship he and his mother shared. As much as he enjoyed talking to his mother he couldn't stay focused on the conversation. Shelby was at the forefront of his mind.

Feeling his mother was satisfied with their conversation, Christian used the time difference as an excuse to end the call. He undressed and went to take a shower.

Hot water beat against Christian's chest and ran down his muscular frame. He stuck his head under the pulsating stream and allowed the water to massage his scalp. No matter how hard he tried to resist, Shelby was having an effect on him. Throughout his life, his mother always encouraged him to get to know people for himself and to never allow another's opinion of a person dictate his feelings towards them. He owed it to Shelby and to himself to see what could happen between them, if anything.

Grabbing a thick towel from the nearby rack, Christian wrapped the towel around his waist and headed into his bedroom. He stared at the cell phone laying on the bedside table and debated about calling Shelby. Although she had given subtle signs, he still was unsure of her interest towards him. Did she really want to get to know him, or was he another one of her conquest? Wrestling back and forth with his thoughts Christian decided to take things slow.

Thanks for inviting me today. I had a great time. Christian sent the text message to Shelby and waited to see if she would reply.

Immediately Christian's phone chimed indicating a new text message.

Thank you for going with me. I'm glad you enjoyed yourself. I had a wonderful time as well.

Christian felt himself relaxing. He wanted to see Shelby again, but he wasn't sure if it was too soon to ask her out. One thing was for sure, if she wasn't feeling the same way he believed she would say so.

Maybe we can get together again sometime. If your schedule permits of course.

Sure, let me know when... She replied

Ok, cool. It's getting late, I'll let you get some rest.

Ttyl goodnight.

Christian put on his pajamas and slid under the covers. He reflected on his trip to Memphis. While Shelby drove through the city streets, Christian made mental notes of things he would like to do on future trips. He was pleased to see the horse drawn carriages. He imagined riding through the city streets with Shelby by his side. Christian also noticed the bright lights on the Orpheum theater sign. He wondered if Shelby was interested in shows and movies.

Based on their conversations throughout the day, Christian could tell Shelby was a woman that enjoyed nice things. If he was going to court her, he needed to be creative.

❄ ❄ ❄ ❄

Shelby placed her phone back on the table. The text message exchange between her and Christian put a huge smile on her face. He wanted to see her again. She was happy she'd made the decision to call him earlier that day. A wave of guilt threatened to rob her of the excitement she felt.

Initially she saw him the same way she viewed all men, as a means to an end. For Shelby it was all about what a man could offer her. She wasn't naïve. She knew she had a reputation as a gold digger. In her opinion, if what people thought was gold digging was going to get her closer to achieving her dream as a fashion designer, then so be it. Contrary to what people thought of her, she was not sleeping with the men she dated. She had become a master at creating a fantasy. Whenever a man reached the point of expecting sex, she found a way to end the relationship.

There was something different about Christian. She felt a connection to him that she had not experienced before. She found him easy to talk to. Initially she could tell he was guarded when it came to her, but all of the walls he had built seemed to crumble when he held her on the dance floor. In her mind, everyone in the room disappeared and the band played for only them. In that moment, nothing and no one else mattered.

Shelby pulled the bedcovers up over her shoulders. With a smile on her face, she nestled into her bed. *Okay Christian, let's see where this goes.*

Chapter Ten

"Somebody's in a great mood," Deborah teased.

Christian looked up from the computer and tilted his head. "Excuse me," he said wondering if Deborah was talking to him or someone else in the office.

"Don't give me that look, Christian. I'm talking to you." Pointing at the radio she continued. "You've got music playing and you keep smiling for no explainable reason. You're in your own little world. What's going on with you today?"

"Nothing's going on," he replied nonchalantly. "I was in the mood for some music so I turned on the radio. No big deal."

Deborah folded her arms across her chest. "No big deal, huh? Okay, we'll go with that. I don't believe it, but we'll go with it."

Laughing off Deborah's inquisition, Christian continued to work. He paused for a moment to consider her probing. Were his actions really that telling? In his opinion, he was not acting any different than he normally did. Waving his hand in dismissal, he attempted to once again focus on work. His efforts were becoming increasingly fruitless.

"I'm going to lunch," Christian announced while logging off of his computer.

"Lunch? Already?" Deborah blurted out with no thought

of masking her surprise. She looked up at the clock on the wall and noted the time. "It's only eleven o'clock. You never go to lunch this early. I would ask if you were feeling all right, but you've been too bubbly this morning not to be."

"Yes, lunch," Christian bit back in a tone that warned Deborah to back off.

"I'm sorry, I meant no offense." Deborah looked at Christian in complete shock. "You have to look over me, I'm known to put my foot in my mouth. The kids say I have no filter."

Christian raised his hands in surrender. "Hey, no offense taken." He looked at his watch, and then back at Deborah. I'll be back in a little while."

Christian walked out of the trailer that served as his makeshift office and descended the four concrete steps. He looked out over the massive lot that would soon house A Mother's Love youth center. Construction of the center was currently underway. Looking at the concrete foundation with metal and PVC piping sticking out of the ground, he visualized the completed center.

He was both honored and humbled by the project. Christian considered the children and families that would be impacted by the center. Stuffing his hand into the front pocket of his dark denim jeans he took in a deep breath and curled his lips up into a slight smile as he exhaled. He pulled his cell phone from his pocket and walked towards his vehicle. Christian waited until he was securely inside the vehicle before initiating the text message he had desired to send all day.

Hello Beautiful, he typed. Pressing the backspace key, he deleted the message and began again. Hey Pretty Lady.

"Ugh," he sighed in frustration, once again deleting the message. "Slow down, Chris, you and Shelby aren't even on that level," he said audibly to himself.

Good morning, Shelby. I hope you're having a good day. Christian pressed the Send key and tossed his phone over to the passenger seat. Turning the key, he put the car in gear and slowly pulled out of the parking lot.

Though he tried to appear frustrated, he knew Deborah had read him like a book. He couldn't believe his actions were that much of a giveaway. Then again, he was working in a small office space with women. He'd learned as a child, women seemed to have a sixth sense. *It must have been that rib God took out of Adam and gave to Eve. That thing must have been a tracking device,* he thought. Laughing at his own joke he proceeded down Main Street in the direction of the nearby city park.

Beep, Beep.

The quick beeps from his cell phone caught Christian's attention. Although he was tempted, he chose to ignore the phone until he was no longer driving. Once he arrived at the park, he pulled in front of the small lake and parked his car.

Reaching over to the passenger side, Christian picked up his phone and viewed the message he had received.

Hey handsome. My day is going great. How are things on your end?

"Oh it's like that," he said, smiling at the display. He didn't want to sound like he was duplicating her message so he chose to omit the flirtatious name calling.

Nothing special, just work, work, work as usual.

You know what they say about all work and no play. Shelby replied.

Yeah, I know. I'm working on that. Christian was hoping his interest in Shelby was evident in his messages.

Looks like you're working on more work. Shelby added a smiling emoji at the end of her message.

I guess you got me there. Christian confessed.

Christian debated about asking Shelby out on an official date. He didn't want to move too fast, but he also didn't want to drag his feet too long. It's not like he was expecting anything long term to come out of seeing her. With him living in Los Angeles that was not a rational thought. On the other hand, he couldn't deny the increased loneliness he was beginning to feel being so far from home. He craved companionship. Spending time with Shelby in Memphis reminded him of what he was indeed missing. He decided to release all of his reservations and to ask her out.

I do need to get out more. What do you say you and I grab some dinner, or catch a movie this evening?

That sounds great, but I can't tonight.

Christian felt a pang of disappointment. He put himself out there and Shelby instantly shot him down. Perhaps he misread the signs he assumed she was throwing out.

Before he could send a response his phone beeped indicating the arrival of another message.

My boss asked me to work late tonight. We're doing inventory. I'm free tomorrow night if you're willing to take a rain check.

Sure, tomorrow night is good. It's no big deal.

Great! I'll call you tomorrow. Enjoy the rest of your day, Christian.

You too, Shelby.

Returning his phone to his pocket, Christian crossed his arms and stared out at the small pond in front of him.

He watched calmly as the ducks swam in a circular pattern. The scene in front of him was serene. He was so caught up in the moment that he almost forgot he was only on a lunch break.

He looked down at the watch he was wearing and noted the time. He had a half hour before he was due back at work. His stomach grumbled reminding him of his decision to skip breakfast.

The small town of Bethany had its advantages, but he missed L.A. Pulling up to the drive-thru window, he ordered a burger and fries along with his usual large Coke. He had become so accustomed to the restaurant that he knew the total before the young man announced it over the speaker. Christian received his order and consumed its contents on the drive back to work. He was growing tired of the routine.

❈ ❈ ❈ ❈

Shelby sat staring at her phone. She couldn't erase the smile that was plastered on her face. The more she thought of Christian, the more excited she became. His timing had been perfect. On the heels of dealing with an irate customer at the boutique his text offered a much needed reprieve.

She hated having to turn down his offer for dinner, especially since things were going so well with them. Their visit to Memphis had gone better than she expected. When she locked her keys in the car at Sunset restaurant he was helpful, but he still seemed a bit stiff. She was pleased to see he was able to relax and be himself. Their time together made her eager to see him again.

There was so much Shelby desired to learn from Christian. She had been around successful men before, but he offered something more. Local men although wealthy were limited in her opinion. Those that chose to leave the area seemed to have a magnet attached to them pulling them back to Bethany.

Unlike her friends and people she had grown up with, Shelby was determined to leave Bethany for good. Her dreams went beyond what she felt the small town could offer. It felt good sharing her dreams with Christian and having him to encourage her. She recalled sharing her dream of being a fashion designer with her friends, family, and men she had dated. She was often met with ridicule and discouragement. It was in those moments that Shelby began to distance herself from both friends and family. She also no longer shared her aspirations with men she dated. That is until Christian came along.

"Excuse me, Miss. I would like to try this dress on." Holding up a black formal gown, the young woman beamed.

"Of course. Right this way." Shelby escorted the young woman to the fitting room.

Shelby watched as the voluptuous teenager tried on dress after dress. With each dress she stood in front of the large mirror feeling defeated.

Approaching the young woman, Shelby felt an overwhelming compassion for her. "You've selected some beautiful gowns to try on. May I ask what the occasion is?"

"I'm going to my senior prom. I have to wear the perfect gown."

Shelby's ears perked up. This was her opportunity to do what she loved. She reached out to the young woman and lifted her chin with her hand.

"Honey, we are going to fix you up today. First of all, you need to step away from these black dresses." Shelby grabbed her by the hand and turned her completely around. Following her assessment, she declared, "I have the perfect dress for you, I'll be right back."

She stepped away briefly and returned with a mint green gown. Extending the dress to the young woman she urged, "Try this on."

The teen looked at the gown and immediately frowned. "This dress is too big. I don't wear this size."

Shelby had already taken note of the size of the dresses she had previously discarded. Shelby knew she had to be careful. She didn't want to make her feel insecure. Being familiar with the designers and the way the dresses were cut she knew that would be the perfect outlet she could use to make her customer more comfortable with the size.

"Sweetheart, please trust me on this. This designer's dresses tend to run small," she lied. "Besides, no one will be looking at the size of the dress. That will be our little secret. Please, just give it a try."

Shelby stood outside by the full length mirror and waited for her customer to exit the dressing room. When the young lady came out, her lips curled up to a full toothy smile.

"You are stunning!" Shelby exclaimed.

Displaying a full smile of her own, the young woman declared, "I love it! It's so beautiful."

She turned around in front of the mirror checking herself out at every angle. The strapless full length mint green Mermaid shaped gown accentuated her curves perfectly. The top of the gown had a sweetheart neckline and a crystal overlaid bodice.

"That dress looks like it was made for you, girl. Hold on a second. We have to complete this look."

Shelby went to the shoe section and picked out a pair of silver heeled strappy sandals with crystal accents, and a matching clutch. Next, she went to the front counter and removed a pair of large double stone crystal earrings that were two and a half inches in length.

Returning to her customer, she waited for the young lady to put on the shoes and earrings. "Okay. Now what do you think?" she asked.

Embracing Shelby, she squealed, "It is absolutely perfect! Thank you so much. I never would have considered this dress if it weren't for you."

The young lady followed Shelby up to the front counter to pay for her items.

"I'm happy I was able to help." Leaning closer she whispered, "Always remember, a woman's size is her secret. Not only in this dress, but in all of your clothes. No matter what you put on, work it like you're on the runway. Confidence is a woman's biggest asset. When you're confident, everyone will take notice."

"I've never looked at it like that, thank you," the young lady replied.

Folding her arms across her chest, Shelby watched the girl and her mother leave the store. Events like this one reminded her of her dream. She was grateful to be working in a fashion environment but it wasn't enough. She wanted to see women Joyfully wearing her designs.

Chapter Eleven

Christian placed headphones over his ears and turned up the volume. The hard beats of the music motivated him during his workout routine. Using twenty-five pound weights he did several reps of alternating bicep curls. Next, he did pull-ups and leg lifts. Once he completed strength training, he ran three miles on the treadmill.

Sweat poured from his head and chest revealing the intensity of his workout. Upon achieving his desired distance, he lowered the pace to stabilize his heart rate. Turning up a bottle of water he took several gulps, consuming the entire bottle.

He grabbed a towel from his bag and wiped away the excess moisture. Finishing up with a few stretches he gathered his belongings and headed back to his apartment. The workout had fulfilled its purpose. He already felt the stress of the day dissipating.

❋ ❋ ❋ ❋

Shelby moved her gearshift to the drive position and pulled away from the curb. She was happy to finally be going home. The day had its ups and downs, but she could honestly say the ups triumphed. Pushing the button located on her car's steering wheel, she activated the hands-free feature for her cellphone. Once she heard the familiar beep she instructed, "Call Christian."

"Calling Christian Tyler," The computerize voice replied.

Gripping the steering wheel, Shelby waited with anticipation for Christian to pick up. She was delighted when she heard his voice through her car's speakers.

"What a pleasant surprise, I was just thinking of you. I take it you're heading home," he said sounding as charming as he could.

The smooth melodious sound of Christian's baritone voice caused butterflies to instantly dance in her stomach.

"As a matter of fact I am. How'd you guess?" Shelby tried to add a bit of seduction in her tone but she was no match for Christian. Her words resembled that of a giddy schoolgirl instead of the vixen she was trying to portray.

"You mentioned you were working late tonight when you texted me earlier. I simply put two and two together."

"I suppose I can add pays attention to your list of qualities," she teased.

"Oh, so you're keeping a list. I hope you have plenty of paper."

"Trust me, I do." Shelby was surprised by Christian's uninhibited flirting. She was quickly realizing she shouldn't make any assumptions when it came to him. More than anything she was hoping he was being authentic. For as long as she could remember men had approached her with what she initially felt were good intentions only to find their motives were all the same.

Christian cut into her thoughts. "How was your day?" he asked sincerely.

"To be honest, it started out pretty crappy. Between irate customers, sassy coworkers, and an impatient boss I was one step from completely losing my cool." Shelby adjusted her tone. "That is until…"

"Until what?" Christian pressed. Shelby had peaked his curiosity.

"Until I got the text from you. Your timing was perfect. In fact, after I received your text my day seemed to turn completely around."

"Is that so?" Christian tried to keep his pride in check. He perceived her attraction for him was increasing.

"Funny how that works, isn't it?" she stated.

Shelby attempted to change the subject. She didn't want to give Christian the wrong impression. Although she was very attracted to him, she was determined to take things slowly.

"I looked at a few movie listings today when I had a free moment. It seems the best movies aren't coming out until Friday."

Recalling their previous text exchange, Christian agreed with her. "I can understand that. Most new movies are released on Friday. I don't know what I was thinking earlier when I invited you to a movie on tonight. I keep forgetting things here aren't like they are in L.A." His frustration became evident in his tone. "It seems this place doesn't come alive until the weekend."

Shelby noticed the change in Christian's voice. She could understand his frustration. There was no way she would have left Los Angeles to come to Bethany. Even though she had been there her entire life, she never felt like she belonged. One thing was for sure, she was determined that whenever she finally got away from there she would only come back for brief visits with her mother.

"Christian, I honestly don't know how you do it. I can't imagine how you could give up all that you have in Los Angeles to come here."

"It's not easy, that's for sure." Christian pondered a thought before continuing. "I'm comforted knowing that I haven't given up anything. When I'm done with this project I'll return home to the life I've worked hard to establish. I also realize my temporary sacrifice is going to produce a long term blessing to everyone who will benefit from the youth center."

Shelby considered his words. "That's a good way to look at things, I suppose."

Turning the key to her front door, she stepped inside her home and kicked her shoes off. She felt relief instantly. Standing in heels all day always had a negative effect on her feet. "Ahhh," she breathed into the phone.

"Are you all right over there?" Christian inquired jokingly.

"Yes I'm fine," Shelby answered laughing. "I just kicked my shoes off. What you heard was my feet saying thank you."

"I don't know how you women do it. I don't even want to imagine not only how, but why you all endure the pain you do."

"We do it because we like the way the male species ogles over us. Don't try to act like you don't like the way a woman's legs look when she is walking in heels."

"You've got a point there. We do enjoy it," he agreed.

Christian and Shelby continued to talk for over an hour. Neither of them was ready to end their conversation. They decided to call it a night when they started passing yawns back and forth.

He was the first to speak up. "I think we better call it a night. If not, we're going to yawn each other to death."

"I have to agree with you. Sleep is threatening to overtake me. I'll talk to you tomorrow." After saying their goodbyes, she pressed the button to disconnect the call.

Shelby enjoyed her conversations with Christian. She felt like she could relax and be herself. Some of the men she had dated in the past expected her to be perfect. If she dared complain about anything she was immediately scolded. They felt their money gave them the power to treat her more like a servant than a companion. It was time for her to dismiss William. He no longer had a place in her life.

She wasn't expecting anything to come out of her spending time with Christian, but she was determined to enjoy the moment. If nothing else, she'll have a story to tell her nosy best friend, Kim.

Chapter Twelve

"Shelby, when you get this message, please give me a call. It's very important that I talk to you. Please call me back today. Okay, bye"

What could she possibly want now? Shelby thought after listening to the message from her younger sister, Sheena. She never called to simply hold a conversation. The only time Shelby heard from her was when she needed something. More times than not, it was money.

It was not Shelby's fault her sister chose to drop out of high school in the middle of her senior year to follow Wendell's behind to New York. he had fed her all of those pipe dreams, telling her he was going to make millions as a rapper. The thought still infuriated Shelby. How could her sister be so stupid? Wendell could barely form complete sentences let alone rap.

Two months later, she was on the phone calling their mother Linda asking for money to get back to Bethany. Shelby watched as her mother sacrificed, even giving up her bill money to bring Sheena home. On top of all of the drama she had already caused, she had lied about the cost of the ticket so that their mother would send enough money to pay for tickets for both of them.

To say that Shelby and Sheena did not have a close relationship would be an understatement. Of the four girls, they clashed the most. Since childhood, their mother had often referred to them as a coin. She said they were permanently joined together but would always be on opposite sides. So far she had been correct.

As a single mother, Linda had done all she could to provide for Shelby and her three sisters. Shelby hated watching her mother struggle. Although her sisters often complained about not being able to go places and have some of the things their friends had, Shelby remained optimistic. She took the clothes her mother bought her from the thrift store and put a new spin on them, often garnering complements.

At one point, Linda was working two jobs while trying to make ends meet. Being the oldest came with a greater set of responsibilities. She was expected to take care of her sisters as well as herself. Now that they were all grown women she figured they should stand on their own. Whatever Sheena's issue was she would have to work it out without her help.

Shelby removed her clothes from the dryer and carried the basket into the living room. Placing the laundry basket on the floor by the couch, she tuned in to her favorite talk show and proceeded to fold her clothes. She chose to use her days off to straighten up around her home.

A loud knock on the door startled her. She was not expecting anyone, but apparently someone was eager to get in.

"Who is it?" she yelled. Stepping closer to the door.

"It's me, Shelby. Open the door."

"I don't believe this." Shelby was infuriated. She opened the door and blocked her sister's path.

"What do you want, Sheena?"

"Dang, it's like that? You're sitting up here blocking the

door and stuff. Who you got up in there?" Sheena stood on her tip toes trying to see inside.

"I don't have anybody in here, and if I did that wouldn't be your business anyway. Now what do you want?" Shelby pressed.

"Stop playing, Shelby." Sheena pushed past her sister and walked into the townhouse. She stepped around the laundry basket and took a seat on the couch. Reaching into the basket of folded clothes she pulled out a white one-shoulder top.

"Ooh, Shelby this is cute. Where did you get this top from?"

"Put my shirt down." Shelby walked around the coffee table and stood facing her sister. "I know you didn't come all the way over here for nothing. What do you want?"

"I came over here because you act like you can't answer nobody's phone call. I know you got my message."

"I've been busy. Now what is so important that you couldn't wait on a returned call?"

"Well," Sheena said dragging her words out. She smacked her lips to add emphasis. "Sis, I need your help."

Rolling her eyes, Shelby gibed, "Imagine that."

Ignoring her sister's sarcasm, Sheena continued her plea. "I need you to let me hold a few dollars until I get my check Friday. My lights are going to get turned off today if I don't pay the bill, and I won't get paid until the end of the week."

"You must be out of your mind. I'm not giving you any money." Shelby placed her hand on her hip and tapped her chin with her other hand. "Come to think of it, you still owe me money from the last time you came over here begging."

"I told you I was going to give you your money back when I get my income tax refund. I haven't forgotten what I owe you."

"Girl please, it is the end of May. You are not about to get any income tax refund this late in the year. If you had a refund coming you have already gotten it and spent it. Don't try to play me for a fool."

"Why are you tripping, Shelby? It's not like you don't have the money. I know about that big settlement you got a while back. Plus, everybody knows about them sugar daddies that be taking care of you."

Shelby was furious. She was well aware of her reputation around town. The last thing she needed was for her sister to throw it up in her face. People assumed they knew her, but they didn't have a clue what was really going on in her life.

"First of all, you don't know what you're talking about. Second of all, I'm tired of you always coming over here begging. The only time I hear from you is when you want something. Maybe if you had the sugar daddy that you assume I have instead of that loser Wendell, then you wouldn't be over here trying to get me to pay your bills. So please, miss me with that." Shelby waved her hand dismissing her sister.

Sheena was furious. She jumped up from the couch and stomped towards the door. "Forget you Shelby, don't nobody need you no way. I don't know why I came over here anyway. You can say what you want about Wendell, but at least I got a man."

"Oh, is that what they're called these days? I thought a man was somebody that could not only take care of himself, but also his woman."

Shelby walked to the door where Sheena was standing with her hand on the doorknob. "Weren't you leaving? I really don't have time for your antics today."

Sheena yelled a string of obscenities before walking out and slamming the door behind her.

Shelby didn't mean to have such a huge fight with her sister. She was tired of Sheena viewing her as an ATM. She had to put a stop to it. That was another reason she wanted to get away. It was time her sisters stood on their own two feet, and got off her back, especially Sheena.

Walking back into the living room Shelby continued folding her clothes. Once she had completed her task, she reached for the bundles and took them to her closet to put them away.

"Ugh!" she yelled pulling her fingers into a tight fist. She couldn't believe she hadn't noticed. "That heifer done stole my shirt!"

Chapter Thirteen

"What's going on, man!" Blake answered Christian's call with excitement.

"It's the same ole, same ole. I'm just here working," Christian replied with unmatched enthusiasm.

"Man, every time I talk to you, you say the same thing. I know you went to Tennessee to work, but if you keep this up—you're going to be miserable."

Christian considered his words. Blake had no idea how true his statement was. He was starting to feel boxed in and he didn't like the man he was turning into. He was focusing so much attention on the building project that he found himself despising it. It seemed as if Christian had no life outside of the youth center.

"Blake, man, you have no idea how hard it is here," he confessed. "I didn't think it would be this bad because you know me, I'm pretty good at adjusting to new situations. I'll admit I wasn't prepared for a change this drastic. This town is so small. There is nothing to do here. If I have to stare at these walls any longer, or watch another round of Sports Center I'm going to lose it."

"Calm down, man. You have gone down there and lost your mind. Chill out."

"Man, I'm telling you, it's this place. It feels like it's sucking the life out of me."

Laughing deviously, Blake replied, "You know what you

need."

"Nah, man, what's that?" Christian pretended to be naive.

"I'm trying to tell you, man. You need some of that good, good."

Christian erupted in laughter. "I should have known you were going there. I swear that's all you think about."

Joining Christian in laughter, Blake continued. "You're laughing but I'm dead serious. If you had a woman, you wouldn't be sitting up crying. Talking about you tired of looking at the walls and Sports Center. You better man up and find you a chick to spend some time with."

"You know what, I'm not even going to lie. I agree it would be nice to have a woman to spend some time with. But, man you know me. I don't believe in meaningless hook-ups with random women. I respect women too much for that."

"So you're telling me for as long as you've been gone you haven't spent time with nobody?"

"I'm not saying all that."

"Man, what! I knew it. You've been holding out on your boy." Blake yelled into the phone. "Somebody's got your nose wide open. Who is she?"

Surrendering, Christian decided to fill his best friend in on his interest in Shelby.

"There's this woman named Shelby. Man, she is fine too. Brown skinned, long wavy hair, pretty brown eyes, and a body any man would love. I'm talking about curves in all the right places."

"Ooh wee. From the way you describe her, I can only imagine what she looks like in person. So what's up with her?"

"She seems pretty cool. Last weekend she invited me to go to Memphis with her. I haven't had that much fun in a long time. I can tell there is a connection between us, but I don't want to take things too fast. You know what I mean?"

Blake considered Christian's words. He could tell his friend really liked this woman, but there was something holding him back from pursuing her.

"What's wrong with her, Chris? I mean you sound like you're feeling her, but at the same time there is something that's got you putting on the breaks."

"See here's the thing. When I first got here, I saw her in a restaurant with some old dude. She was laughing and rubbing his hand. In fact, it was her laugh that caught my attention. She has one of those laughs that will make you laugh without even knowing what's funny."

Christian paused for a moment, switching his phone from one hand to the other before continuing.

"I was there with several members of the board of directors for the youth center. When this dude named Thaddeus saw me looking at her, he basically told me not to waste my time with her because she was a gold digger."

"Ah, man," Blake interjected. "You don't need to go there then. You don't want a repeat of Alexia. That girl took you through some serious changes. All she was about was what you could do for her."

"I know. Trust me, I'm not trying to go down that path again."

Christian shook his head at the memory. He knew it wouldn't be fair to judge Shelby based on his history with Alexia. He needed to tell Blake the rest of the story. In the event something developed between him and Shelby, he didn't want Blake to have a negative opinion of her without getting to know her.

"Here's the thing. When she invited me to go to Memphis. I wanted to get out of this little town so bad that I gladly accepted her invitation. Man, all I can say is, I haven't had that much fun in a long time."

"You said that already." Blake took a deep breath, and let it out slowly. Aw man, Chris, it sounds like you've got it bad."

"To tell you the truth, I haven't stopped thinking about her since that day. She seems like a good woman."

Blake didn't want to discourage his friend. The sadness that he detected in Christian's tone when they began their conversation had completely disappeared once he started talking about Shelby.

"Have you seen her anymore since then?" Blake asked.

"No, I haven't seen her, but we have either texted or talked practically every day since. We're planning to get together again this weekend.

"I can tell you really like this chick because your whole tone changed when you started talking about her. All I have to say is keep your eyes open, man. Take it slow. Don't get so caught up that you lose focus. Just have some fun. Don't over think it. After all you live on the other side of the country. You're just trying to pass the time."

"Thanks Blake. I know you're right, and I appreciate that."

"No problem man, that's what I'm here for. Make sure you keep me posted. Especially if you get some of that country trim." Blake laughed at his own comment.

"Dawg, you're stupid. I don't think you're capable of thinking of anything else. But you're my boy, and I love you."

"Listen, Chris man, I need to get off this phone. I have some stuff I need to take care of. Don't forget what I said."

Christian was glad he talked to Blake about Shelby. It was always good to talk to his friend, and he reminded him to keep his focus. He owed it to Shelby to give her the benefit of the doubt. He was more eager than ever for their date. It was time for him to plan it out.

Chapter Fourteen

The bed was littered with an array of colors: red, turquoise, black, purple. Tossing a white dress onto the bed, Shelby added it to the growing pile of discarded garments. Standing in front of her full length mirror, she held up a yellow dress.

"Ugh! No, no, no," she yelled in frustration. "This should not be this difficult."

She added the yellow dress to the pile. Feeling defeated, she sat down on the bed and peered into her closet. Her eyes lit up when they fell on the perfect dress. Smiling broadly, she skipped over to the closet and grabbed the dress. "I can't believe I didn't see this before."

❀ ❀ ❀ ❀

Christian followed the directions Shelby had given him to her home. He smiled as he recalled her words during their previous telephone conversation. "You'll never learn your way around if you're always depending on that navigation system." She had no idea just how true that statement had been for him.

Right on schedule he arrived at her townhouse. He pulled into the driveway and turned off the engine. Christian was thrilled about his date with Shelby. He had worked hard to plan what he felt would be a fun filled evening. The only thing he'd told her was they would be leaving Bethany.

Although he was not completely familiar with the area, he knew enough about it to know there was not much to do in Bethany.

Before exiting the vehicle, Christian grabbed the small gift he had for her from the passenger side.

His nerves threatened to get the best of him as he approached the front door. Taking a deep cleansing breath, he pulled air into his lungs and exhaled slowly. Reaching out, he tapped on the door and waited.

He didn't have to wait long.

Shelby swung the door open almost immediately.

"Wow, you look amazing," Christian said, scanning Shelby from head to toe.

She wore a royal blue low cut wrap dress that stopped mid-thigh. Her hair was pinned up on one side. On her neck she wore a bright yellow necklace in the shape of various length flowers along with matching earrings. The flower in the middle of the necklace stopped just above her full bust. Her shapely legs were long and inviting. Her feet were adorned in bright yellow kitten heeled sandals revealing a royal blue pedicure with small flowers.

"Thank you. You don't look bad yourself."

Shelby was pleased with the maroon, button down shirt he wore opened at the collar. He had his sleeves flipped up on the end revealing a black Cartier Roadster watch. His black slacks fit like they were tailor made, sitting atop polished black Bally loafers.

She invited Christian inside. "Is that for me?" Shelby asked laughing at Christian's sudden case of amnesia and laryngitis.

Finding his voice, Christian answered, "Yes it is." He extended the single long stemmed orange rose to her.

"I don't believe I've ever seen an orange rose before. This is beautiful and it smells divine." Placing her hand on her hip, she continued, "I also don't believe I've gotten only one rose. Is that how it's done in Los Angeles?"

"No, that's not how it's done in L.A. This is our first official date and by giving you one rose I leave room for growth. If I start you off with a full dozen, you won't have anything to look forward to. As for the color, it has a meaning of its own."

"You are too deep," she replied jokingly. Placing her nose slightly above the rose, she inhaled deeply, admiring the unusual fruity essence. "I'm going to put this in some water, and grab my bag. I'll be ready to go in a second."

Shelby walked swiftly into the kitchen and pulled a vase from the cabinet. She placed the lone rose inside and moved into the bedroom to retrieve her handbag.

"All set," she declared after re-joining Christian who was still waiting by the door.

Christian walked around to the passenger side to open the door for Shelby. Once she was secure inside, he stepped around to the driver's side and joined her. He was quietly hoping the night he had planned would go smoothly. Turning on the navigation system, he pressed the preprogramed key for the movie theater.

"There you go with that navigation system," Shelby teased.

"You leave Lucy alone," Christian replied pretending to be offended.

"You gave it a name. Wow," Shelby laughed.

"Yes, I gave her a name. You're just mad because I'm listening to another woman."

Christian and Shelby looked at each other and started

laughing all over again. Their date was starting off on a joyful note as Christian had hoped it would. If everything continued to go as planned, he would get to see that beautiful smile Shelby displayed, all night long.

Shelby watched in delight as Christian skillfully tackled the highway. He drove as if he were a local resident. Subtly she admired the definition in his arms. His muscles flexed when he gripped the steering wheel causing her heartbeat to elevate slightly.

"Now that we're all dressed up, what do you have planned for us?" she asked.

"I figured we would start off the night with a movie, and then afterwards I have a surprise for you."

Smiling her approval, Shelby replied, "I like surprises, especially good ones."

Nodding his head in agreement, Christian smiled. "I'll be honest with you, I've been looking forward to this night all week. I'm starting to feel a bit homesick. The fact that the only people I know are mainly people involved with the building project doesn't help either. One thing is for sure, it doesn't offer much of an escape. I enjoy your company, and I knew spending time with you would be a great cure for the blues."

On one hand, Shelby wanted to offer a comforting shoulder. However, she didn't want to be treated like a placeholder. She didn't want loneliness to be the only reason Christian spent time with her. With mixed feelings, she decided to get to know him better.

"Tell me about your life in Los Angeles, what's it like living in Hollywood?"

"L.A. is cool. I wouldn't call where I live Hollywood by any stretch of the imagination. Much like New York, it's a city the never sleeps. There are a lot of dreamers there. Pretty much everywhere you go, you find people that are desperately hoping to be discovered. It seems everyone has a headshot from the restaurant servers, to the building security guards. I personally never wanted a life in the limelight."

While Christian spoke, Shelby painted a mental picture of Los Angeles. She imagined sitting in a restaurant and having the server bring a copy of their headshot along with the check. She wondered if there were people sitting on street corners performing monologues, the way New Yorkers sing on the subway.

"Do you have many friends back home? Are you close to your family?" she asked.

"I have a few friends, most of which are business associates. My closest friend is my buddy Blake. He and I have been friends since childhood. We're tight like brothers."

"That sounds like me and my girl, Kim. Although I have three younger sisters, Kim and I have always been extremely close since we were in elementary school. My dad left when we were still little and my mother had to work hard to take care of us. Since I'm the oldest, I had the most responsibility looking after my sisters. My friendship with Kim helped me to get through it. When she came around, and we hung out together I was able to focus on myself."

"Wow, three sisters. That's a big family. I'll bet your house was always busy. It's good you had Kim in your life. From what I hear, being the oldest is not an easy task. I'm an only child, so I missed out on all of the sibling rivalry. There were some lonely days. Many times I wished I had siblings. My father was the type that liked to pop in and out of our lives. He never offered my mother anything. Since my mother had a fairly decent job she didn't press the issue. She always said a strong woman never begs anyone to take care of her. She goes out and makes it happen."

"I guess in some ways; we have more in common than we imagined." Shelby acknowledged.

"It appears so," Christian replied.

Christian drove the length of the parking lot, row after row searching for an open spot. "They must really have some good movies playing tonight, this parking lot is packed."

Shelby pointed out an open space a few feet ahead of them. "This is the newest and most popular movie theater in Jackson. They have the most screens and they show the movies the vast majority want to see, so people mainly come here."

"Oh, I see."

Christian pulled into the open space and turned off the engine. Climbing out of the driver's seat, he walked over to Shelby's side and opened the door. Extending his arm to her he asked playfully, "Shall we?"

Stepping out of the car, Shelby grabbed a hold of his arm. "We shall."

Once he'd purchased their tickets, they went inside. Shelby headed into the ladies' room to freshen up while Christian proceeded to the snack counter to get refreshments.

He stood in line and peered at the offerings. He was so focused on the task at hand that he didn't notice the familiar face approaching him.

"Hey, Christian, what's up, man?"

Christian extended his hand offering the man a handshake. "Hey, how're you doing?"

"I'm good. I'm surprised to see you here. I didn't think you ever left that building site."

"I'm here enjoying a night out, much like yourself," he added pointing to the man's female companion.

Shelby returned from the ladies' room eager to join Christian. She noticed him talking to a man and woman but she couldn't make out their identities because their backs were to her.

Christian smiled broadly when he saw her approaching, causing the man to immediately turn in her direction.

"Shelby," the man said flatly giving her a look of disgust.

"Thaddeus," she replied sharply.

Giving Christian a piercing stare, Thaddeus, abruptly ended his visit. "Enjoy your movie," he said as he and his female companion walked away.

Christian could see the intense dislike Shelby and Thaddeus had for one another through their exchange. *What's up with that?* He wondered. Whatever the issue between Thaddeus and Shelby was it would have to wait. Tonight belonged to he and Shelby and nobody was going to ruin it.

"All right, beautiful, let's get these snacks before our movie starts."

Shelby offered Christian a smile that didn't reach her eyes. Walking up seeing him talking to Thaddeus gave her a sick feeling in the pit of her stomach. She wasn't sure if Christian could see the dislike they had for each other. Who was she kidding? Even a blind man could have seen the hatred in their eyes. She could only hope Thaddeus wasn't poisoning Christian with his lies about her.

Let it go, Shelby. Don't allow Thaddeus to have this power over you. Wrestling with her thoughts, Shelby struggled to refocus her attention on Christian and their date. Thaddeus Bierman was like a cancer to her. He always seemed to pop up where he wasn't wanted.

Christian could no longer ignore Shelby's reclusion. She and Thaddeus obviously had some history that caused ill feelings on both ends. He found himself in a tough position. If he didn't say something the rest of their night could go poorly. Then again, if he said something, he wasn't sure how she would react.

Stopping mid stride, Christian turned to Shelby. "Listen, I don't know what the deal is with you and Thaddeus, and I'm not asking. I brought you here to have a good time. I'm not going to let nothing and no one interfere with that."

Scanning her body from head to toe, he added. "Besides, you are looking too good to be upset. Now, let me see that gorgeous smile of yours."

A broad smile appeared on Shelby's lips. She was so impressed by Christian. He seemed like he genuinely cared about her feelings. The men she dated in the past would have ignored her feelings and continued on as if nothing had happened. For this reason alone, she owed him her attention.

❀ ❀ ❀ ❀

"I'm glad you chose a comedy. I love to laugh. Kevin Hart is a fool. He's so funny." Shelby was still laughing as they walked out of the theater.

"I know what you mean. I love his movies. I always wonder how much of what he says and does is a part of the script. I personally think he does a lot of improvisation,"

Christian added.

"I'd have to agree with you on that. Especially with the way some of his co-stars react. They look like they are holding back laughs big time," Shelby agreed.

Christian excused himself and headed into the restroom. Once they were back inside the car, he started the ignition and turned to Shelby. "Are you ready for part two?"

Shelby pursed her lips and pouted. "I am if it involves food. Shoot, I'm hungry."

"It does," he replied, mimicking her pouting. "I found this place online. Based on the reviews, I believe you'll enjoy it."

A short drive later they arrived at Grooves Gallery, a restaurant that featured live Jazz musicians. The atmosphere was welcoming and sensual. Round tables were placed throughout the dining area. They were decorated with burgundy tablecloths and wide black table runners. Small fishbowl shaped vases contained tea light candles. Plush burgundy velvet chairs were placed around each table.

The front of the restaurant featured a full jazz band rendering soulful sounds. They were immediately greeted by a man wearing a black suit with a burgundy vest and bowtie.

"Good evening, sir, ma'am. Do you have reservations?"

Christian placed his hand at the small of Shelby's back. "Yes we do. Our reservation is listed under Christian Tyler."

"Ah, yes Mr. Tyler. I see you requested a table near the dance floor. We have your table ready. Right this way. The host escorted Christian and Shelby to a table at the front of the restaurant aligned with the center of the stage.

Once they were seated, he turned his attention to Christian. "As you requested, sir." He then poured each of them a glass of Dom Pérignon from the bottle chilling in the ice bucket on the table.

"Your meals will be out momentarily." The host nodded his head at Christian and headed back towards the front of the restaurant.

Shelby looked at Christian with both amazement and confusion. Taking a sip of champagne, she expressed her delight with a soft moan. "This is very nice, Christian. I'm a little confused though. He said our meals will be out, but we haven't ordered anything yet."

Christian gave a subtle smile. His plans were coming together the way he'd imagined. "I hope you don't mind. I took the liberty of placing our orders ahead of time."

"Okay, I can't wait to see what you selected. Judging by how everything else is turning out, I expect nothing short of amazing."

Shelby and Christian swayed to the music while they awaited their meals. A tall slender man was playing a saxophone solo, drawing them in with every note.

Towards the end of the song, as promised, their server appeared wearing a black shirt and slacks. Topping off her outfit, was a burgundy bowtie and small black apron.

Placing the plates down in front of them, she announced, "For you this evening, we have our hand carved filet mignon, and blackened Maine lobster tail. If you need anything, my name is Ayonna. Enjoy your meal."

"Wow! This looks delicious." Shelby stared into Christian's eyes, "I can't believe you did all of this for me."

Christian felt an overwhelming since of pride. The woman sitting in front of him was not only beautiful, but she also appeared genuinely surprised and happy. Returning her intent stare, he saw what he perceived as sincere gratitude in her eyes.

"I'm honored to do this for you, Shelby. Every woman deserves to be wined and dined. Besides, I had to make a lasting impression. I hope I've done that tonight."

"You most certainly have, Christian. Thank you."

Christian watched in delight as Shelby swayed to the smooth melodies permeating throughout the restaurant. She sliced off a small piece of steak and placed it in her mouth. Closing her eyes, she devoured the succulent dish.

"Ummm, this is delicious," she declared between bites. "I can't believe I've never heard of this place."

"I'm glad I was able to show you something new."

Although he spoke in reference to the restaurant, Christian was hoping Shelby caught on to the unspoken clues he was giving. He tried hard to hide the feelings he was developing for her, but that was increasingly becoming more difficult with each moment they spent together.

The two continued to share easy conversation while they dined. They talked about everything from school mascots to childhood dreams.

Shelby wiped her mouth with the cloth napkin and placed it on the table. The band played the beginning of Johnny Gill's song, *My My My*.

"Ooh, that's my jam," she said, rocking in her chair more than before.

"Are you going to keep using that chair as your dance partner, or will you do me the honor of having this dance?" Christian stood and extended his hand to her.

"Hmm, you or the chair. How's a woman to choose," Shelby joked. Placing her hand in his, she rose from her seat and followed Christian to the dance floor.

He pulled her close. Intertwining her fingers with his, he placed his other hand at the small of her back. Their hips swayed in perfect unison as they moved to the slow rhythm.

Shelby laid her head on Christian's chest, closed her eyes and allowed the music to envelop her. She could feel his arm tighten around her waist. While they danced, it felt like they shared a heartbeat. She wanted him to be hers. Releasing his hand, she placed her arms around his neck and savored the moment.

The song ended, but Christian remained in place holding her in his arms. She looked up to find him peering into her eyes. Returning his gaze, they stood in complete silence. In any other situation Shelby would have felt awkward, but at that moment. Everything felt right. She let herself go and relaxed in his arms.

Christian tightened his embrace. The song they danced to expressed his feelings completely. He felt a connection to Shelby like he had never experienced before. Looking into her eyes, he saw himself. Her eyes revealed what her mouth had not spoken. Shelby was a woman that desired to be loved and appreciated. For him, distance no longer mattered. In his arms with her body pressed against his was a woman he could share his love and his life with. He didn't care what anyone said or thought, he refused to let this opportunity slip away.

Releasing his arms from her back, Christian let go of all inhibitions and held Shelby's face in his hands. With expressed desire he covered her mouth with his and kissed her passionately.

Chapter Fifteen

"My my my…" Shelby danced around the house singing the song from the restaurant. She was still relishing in her evening with Christian. Never in her wildest dreams had she imagined the stranger from Los Angeles would sweep her off her feet like a fairytale prince charming.

In a short span of time she had developed feelings she could not explain where Christian was concerned. She placed her hand on her lips, recalling the passion of the kiss they shared. They were so in tune with one another that she had almost forgotten they were standing in the middle of the dance floor.

Being with Christian made her feel like a different life was possible. Kicking off her shoes, she headed to her bedroom to change clothes. The phone rang, drawing her attention to the present. She quickly pressed the answer key.

"Hello," she said in a sensual tone. She figured Christian must have made it to his apartment by now.

"You sure did look good in that sexy blue dress. All I could think about was how much I wanted to tap that."

"Who is this?" Shelby yelled into the phone.

"Don't act like you don't recognize my voice. You know exactly who this is, gold digger."

"How dare you call my phone, and you have the nerve

to try to insult me. How did you get my phone number, Thaddeus? You low life jerk. Don't ever call me again."

"I call it like I see it. Don't worry about how I got your phone number. All you need to know is I have friends in high places. You think you're going to get your claws into Christian. Well you're not, I'm going to make sure he knows exactly who and what you are."

"I'm not afraid of you, Thaddeus. You're nothing but a coward. You need to get a life and stop focusing on me. You're just mad because you can't have me. You don't know anything about my relationship with Christian, so back off. Now for the last time, don't contact me ever again, or I will handle you."

Thaddeus laughed wickedly. "Trust me my dear, this isn't over. You may as well get ready."

"Ugh, I hate him!" Shelby yelled after disconnecting the call. Thaddeus was a living, breathing thorn. Christian Tyler was her opportunity for happiness, and there was no way she would allow Thaddeus or anyone else to ruin it for her.

❀ ❀ ❀ ❀

Christian tossed his keys on the kitchen counter and pulled a glass out of a nearby cabinet. He pressed the glass against a small lever and extracted cold water from the refrigerator. He turned the glass up and took a big gulp. Holding his arm up to his nose, Christian inhaled deeply. He smiled when he realized he could still smell Shelby's perfume from when he held her close.

The night had been all that Christian expected and more. He liked the way he and Shelby looked as a couple. Inwardly he hoped something positive would come of their time spent together. The reality of him living in Los Angeles hung over his head like a storm cloud. There was no way he would give up his life in California, and he didn't feel comfortable asking her to give up her life in Tennessee.

Taking another gulp of water, he willed himself to slow down. Two dates with a woman didn't equal a relationship. The last thing he needed to do was to move too fast. He also couldn't ignore the exchange between Shelby and Thaddeus. There was definitely more to that story, and he owed it to himself to find out what wasn't being said.

Christian drained the remnants of his glass and headed into his bedroom. Pulling his phone from his pocket, he checked to see if he had a message from Shelby. Disappointed, he tossed the phone onto the bed. After changing into his pajamas, he slid under the covers. He laid motionless with his arm behind his head, and stared at the ceiling, replaying the evening with Shelby in his mind. He couldn't get over how beautiful she was. That blue dress hugged her curves in all the right places. Her makeup looked like it had been applied professionally, and the smell of her perfume made him want to devour her.

He'd gone all out for their date and he was so glad he had. The passion of their kiss showed him Shelby was as attracted to him, as he was to her. She'd even reached for his hand in the car and held onto it until they arrived back at her home. Not wanting to do too much too fast, he opted to kiss her on her hand as they parted ways.

Christian's cellphone chimed, immediately drawing his attention.

Thank you for a wonderful evening. I can't express in words how much I enjoyed myself. XOXO Shelby

His lips instantly turned up into a smile. Tapping the

screen, he eagerly replied.

It was my pleasure. I enjoyed spending the evening with you. Looking forward to the next time.

Me too, she replied adding smiley face emojis.

Goodnight beautiful, I hope you sleep well.

You too, Christian. Goodnight.

Christian plugged his phone into the charger and turned over. He offered up a silent prayer asking for guidance. He didn't want to walk into an unforeseen trap. Although Blake had advised him to keep things casual, he wasn't that type of man. He put his heart into everything he did, which is why more than ever he needed to move slowly.

Chapter Sixteen

Linda answered the door with joy. She extended her arm and pulled her daughter into a loving embrace. "Well isn't this a surprise. Come on in here, girl."

Shelby wrapped her arms around her mother in a loving embrace. Linda stepped aside so that she could enter. Shelby headed straight for the kitchen.

"Mama, what are you cooking? Something smells good."

"The ladies at the church have been on me about my pies. I decided to fix some to take to church tomorrow."

"How many pies are you baking?" Shelby looked around at the pies on the countertop and the table. Several pies were already done and there appeared to be more that still needed to be baked.

Linda smiled broadly. "I baked twelve sweet potato pies and eight pecan pies."

Shelby gave her mother a sidelong glance. "Really, Mama. You fixed twenty pies?"

"What's wrong with that? Honey, them folks at church love my pies. Shoot these will be gone before I get in the building good."

"Whatever you say, Mama." Shelby teased. Picking up one of the pies, she looked at her mother and declared, "I'll take this one off your hands. You can take them the other nineteen."

"Girl, you better put that pie back."

"Mama!"

"Grab you one of those out of the freezer. They're just as good."

Shelby turned her lips up at her mother and shook her head. "Okay fine, but you ain't right, Mama."

She laughed as her mother sashayed over to the freezer and pulled out a sweet potato pie.

Looking over her shoulder at Shelby, Linda asked, "Are you hungry? I grilled some chicken earlier and I was just getting ready to eat. You're welcome to join me."

"Yes ma'am, you ain't said nothing but a word." Shelby grabbed two plates from the cabinet and filled them with grilled chicken, potato salad, baked beans, and macaroni and cheese.

Realizing Shelby also had prepared her plate, Linda thanked her and offered her a glass of tea. The ladies took their food to the dining room table and sat down.

Linda consumed a forkful of potatoes and washed it down with a sip of tea. "I'm happy to see you, baby."

"I'm happy to see you too, Mama. Somehow I hear a but coming."

"You sure do know your mama. You're not the only one though, because I certainly know my child. When are you going to tell me what's really on your mind? We both know you're not the one for casual visits."

"Wow, Mama. Can we at least finish eating first?" Shelby peeled off a piece of chicken and devoured it. "What's been going on with you?"

Linda knew whatever was on Shelby's mind was pretty major. She was okay with them finishing their meal first. Shelby was such a wild card. Linda figured she would probably need the extra weight from the food to hold her down.

After several minutes of forks tapping against plates Linda spoke up. "Sheena came by here the other day. She had on the cutest white blouse. It looked like something one of those Braxton girls would wear. It looked good on her."

"I'll bet it did. That's the shirt she stole from me when she came to my house." Shelby was furious.

"Are you sure? Sheena may have done a lot of things, some I know about and some I don't. However, I have a hard time believing she stole from you."

"Mama, you have to be kidding. I wouldn't make up something like that. In fact, I can describe it, if you want me to."

"That's not necessary. You girls are sisters. You're supposed to help one another, not tear each other down. Now, I'm not the one to uphold y'all in your wrong. If she took your blouse, then I'll tell her to return it."

"I don't want it back. She knows she was wrong. That's why I haven't heard anything else from her. Sheena makes me sick." Shelby rolled her eyes, showing her displeasure with her sister.

"Shelby, stop all of that. It is not that serious. I'm sure you have plenty more blouses to wear. Help me clear this table. I tell you the truth, you and that sister of yours will be the death of me. You girls act like you can't get along if it saved your life."

"Quit getting yourself all upset for nothing, Mama. Besides, that's not what I came over here for anyway. I need your advice."

Linda looked at her eldest daughter with compassion.

"Baby, what's going on?" Wrinkles were etched across her forehead revealing her concern.

"It's nothing bad. I want to talk to you about this guy I met. We've only gone out a few times, but I'm really starting to like him."

"Let's go in the living room and sit down. This guy must really be something special because this is not like you at all."

Shelby followed her mother and took a seat on the couch. She was developing feelings for Christian and she didn't know what to do about it. Shelby had become accustomed to having casual, meaningless involvements. None of the men she was used to dealing with were relationship material.

Linda settled into her favorite chair, and smiled at her daughter. She rocked gently back and forth. "Tell me about this man of yours."

"I wouldn't call him my man per se. We have only gone out a few times. His name is Christian Tyler. He's a building contractor from Los Angeles."

"Los Angeles!" Linda interrupted. "What in the world is he doing in Bethany?"

"He's working on that big youth center they're building."

"The one that they had all of those fundraisers for?"

"Yes, ma'am, that's the one. Anyway I have gone out with him a few times. We talk or text each other all the time. Mama, every time I'm with him or around him I see myself being with him. He seems to be a great guy."

"Slow down, Shelby. I mean you have to think about this. You already said he's from Los Angeles. What is he going to do when the building is finished? I know he's not going to leave L.A. for a life in Bethany. To do so, would be ridiculous."

"I know, Mama. That's why it's so crazy. As bad as I want to build something with him, I know these no good folks in Bethany won't let us be happy together anyway."

"Why would you say that? In fact, why are you worried about what somebody else says you can or can't have? You are a grown woman. Can't nobody control your life."

"Yeah I know that, but Thaddeus Bierman is on the board of directors. He works with Christian and he's trying to put stuff in his head about me."

"That man really needs to get a life. That case you had against him was years ago. Everybody has moved on past that except him." Linda's anger was evident.

"I know it. He even had the nerve to call me one night after he saw me and Christian out on a date. He wouldn't tell me how he got my number. I'd hate to have to change my phone number all because of him, but I will."

"Honestly Shelby, if you want peace in this situation then you need to talk to Christian. Let him know the real deal, so that there is no room for mess."

"But what if he doesn't believe me. What if Thaddeus gets to him before I do? I don't trust those Bierman's. Unfortunately, they have a lot of pull in this stupid town." Shelby shook her head in frustration. A big part of her felt like she was in a no win situation.

Linda looked at her daughter as if she was seeing a stranger. "Chile, I don't know who this man is, but honey you've got it bad. I've never seen you act like this over anyone. Don't get me wrong. I'm happy that you've found someone that you actually see a future with. However, I don't like the fact that you've lost your fight."

"I haven't lost my fight." Shelby countered.

"Oh yes, you most certainly have. Anytime you come up in here letting anything Thaddeus Bierman has said or done get the best of you, I know something is wrong. You better get up and dust yourself off, and act like the woman I raised you to be."

Linda was adamant in her response. She had always taught her daughters to stand up for themselves. It was that teaching that caused Shelby to fight back when Thaddeus tried to use his position and wealth as a means to take advantage of her.

"Mama you're right. I don't know why I'm tripping off Thaddeus. I honestly can't believe I let him take me there."

"He should be the least of your worries." Linda stopped rocking and sat on the edge of her chair. "You need to guard your heart."

"What are you talking about, Mama?" Shelby asked.

"I'm talking about, Christian. If you fall in love with that man, what's going to happen when it comes time for him to leave? I mean seriously, he lives on the other side of the country. California ain't no hop, skip, and a jump away."

Shelby pretended to be irritated, but in reality she was not ready to face that issue yet. "I know, Mama. I guess I'll cross that bridge when I come to it."

Linda resigned. "You're a smart girl. I'm sure you'll figure something out." Standing she extended her arm to Shelby and helped her up. "Come in here and help me put these pies in the containers."

"Yes Ma'am."

Chapter Seventeen

Shelby stretched the blanket out over the grass near the lake. A gentle breeze forced small waves to ripple in the water.

Opening the basket, Christian placed on the blanket beside her, she carefully removed the contents. Although they were on the ground, Shelby prepared the spread as if they were at a dining table. She laid clear plastic plates and forks in front of Christian and then herself.

Next she placed grilled chicken sandwiches on each plate. Removing a Ziploc bag from her basket she scooped out portions of a watermelon and cucumber salad. Lastly, she added potato salad to each plate. Once she was satisfied with the placement of their meals, she removed two bottles of semi frozen strawberry lemonade and handed one to Christian.

"Everything looks delicious. I can't believe you went through all of this trouble." Christian admired the spread in front of him.

"Thank you, but it was no trouble. I've always wanted to do something like this. I never had the opportunity until now."

"Really?" Christian asked in amazement.

"Yes, really. Now make sure you save room, because I also brought dessert."

Christian did not want to skirt past the revelation she

had revealed to him. He pressed further. "Shelby, you are a beautiful woman, I can't believe you've never been on a picnic. Besides you're here in the country. There's not much else to do around here."

Folding her arms across her chest Shelby replied, "There you go with that city boy, country girl stuff. You've been here long enough to know we don't spend our days harvesting crops and fishing until dusk. We have the same modern conveniences that you have in Los Angeles, we just don't have as many shops and activities. Don't get mad because we have clear air, and we can see our stars in the sky and not on television."

Reaching out to her, Christian pulled Shelby into an embrace. "I'm sorry sweetheart, I didn't mean to offend you. I guess I find it hard to believe that no man has ever done this for you, or you for him." He felt comfortable using the term of endearment.

"Contrary to what you may have heard or believe, I haven't been in many relationships. In fact, I have only had one serious relationship. It lasted four years and after all was said and done, I found out I was in it by myself. I didn't mean as much to him as I thought. I was the only one in love. He accepted what I had to offer, but gave me nothing in return."

"It's his loss, sweetheart. Any man that would treat you the way he did, didn't deserve you."

Shelby offered him a slight nod, before focusing her attention back on her meal. Using a plastic fork, she pushed the food around on her plate.

"What about you, Christian. I'm sure you've been in love a few times in your life."

Christian considered her words. He debated over

telling her about Alexia. In his experience it wasn't usually a good idea to tell women he was interested in about their relationship. Somehow this felt different. Christian believed he was building something special with Shelby. If their relationship was going to be meaningful it would have to start with honesty.

Taking a sip from his bottle of strawberry lemonade, Christian laid aside his reserve, and told Shelby the story of his and Alexia's relationship.

"I had one serious relationship a few years ago with a woman named, Alexia. She and I met in high school and we were good friends. We lost touch during college. Around five years ago we reconnected, when my best friend Blake was dating her best friend, Samantha."

Shelby adjusted herself on the blanket and leaned back on her right elbow. "Go on."

"We started dating and the rest is history." Christian stretched his hands out on both sides emphasizing his point.

"Stop playing Christian. I can take it, tell me what happened."

During our relationship, I had a feeling that she wasn't really in it as much as I was. My mother pressed me concerning the relationship, but I dismissed her concerns. I figured she was being over protective because I'm her only child. You know what they say about a mother and her son."

Shelby nodded her head in understanding.

"It's all true, every bit of it. My mother is so protective of me. That's probably why Alexia was my only serious relationship. I mean I dated others but I was never serious about any of the young ladies the way I was about her."

Christian swallowed a gulp of his beverage. "Back to what I was saying. I could tell something was off, so I showed her more love, hoping she would start to share the feelings. She pretended to do so. In fact, she got to the point that she always wanted to spend time together. From that came her desire to take trips to exotic regions. I loved her so nothing was off limits. My business was successful, I had a beautiful woman that I thought loved me, so why not."

He paused for a moment as if he was re-living the events all over again. "I thought she was the woman I would spend the rest of my life with. Eventually, I proposed. I should have known something was wrong by the look of disgust she gave me when I got down on one knee. Of course that look quickly changed when she saw the ring I held in front of her. She accepted my proposal that night."

Shelby watched as Christian's eyes displayed his anger. He didn't appear angry to the point that she felt concerned. The more she looked at him, she realized what she saw was more hurt than anger. Part of her wished she hadn't pressed him to tell the story. The other part of her was glad she did. She figured the way he handled his past relationships was a good indication of how he might treat her.

"Soon after the proposal, she insisted I purchase her a car. She said it wouldn't be right for my wife to drive less than the best. Once I'd purchased the car, she started in on a condo in Beverly Hills. I was like her genie in a bottle. Her wish was my command."

Shelby listened as Christian outlined the things he had given Alexia. She thought about all the times she had been called a gold digger because of the class of men she'd dated. Their assessment of her couldn't have been further from the truth. The things she had, she worked for. Sure men bought her gifts and gave her cash on occasion, but it was nothing like the money Christian had spent.

Christian could tell, Shelby was slightly distracted, but he needed to get this out, so that it would never be brought up again. "The week before the wedding Alexia was adamant about me staying away from the condo. We had been living there together for close to a year, but she said it would be bad luck for our marriage if I was there during the week leading up to our wedding. I didn't agree with it, but I went along with it. She and I spoke constantly throughout the week up until the night before the wedding."

Sitting up straight on the blanket, Christian devoured the remnants of his lemonade. "On the day of the wedding, I took my place at the altar and awaited my bride. Seconds turned to minutes, and minutes turned into an hour. I looked out at our friends and families and wondered what was keeping her. I pictured every scenario in my mind. Finally, the pastor leaned over and said, it was time for me to accept what had happened. She wasn't coming."

"Wow," was all Shelby could say. She would never do some of the things Alexia had done to Christian. "So that's how it ended. Man, that's deep. I'm sorry you had to go through that. I'm sure it's changed your view of women."

"I would be lying if I said it didn't. I was bitter for a long time. A couple of years later, I was leaving a business meeting and I saw her with some of her friends. I invited her to have coffee with me, so that I could get some answers. She accepted my invitation. During our conversation she apologized to me for the way she'd handled things. She also told me I was partly to blame. She said I knew she didn't love me, but I chose to ignore it. I realized I had to face the truth of her words."

"Have you been in a relationship since then?" Shelby asked.

"I've dated off and on, but nothing serious. In my opinion, casual dating is fine for some, but I want something deeper."

Shelby debated about whether or not to probe him any further, but her curiosity got the best of her. She needed to know if Alexia was still a threat. "What ever happened to her, Christian?" she asked.

Christian could tell Shelby was trying to size up his relationship with Alexia. He decided to put her mind at ease. "The last I heard, she was pursuing a career in modeling and acting. I've seen her on a few commercials, but that's about it. She and I haven't seen or talked since I invited her out for coffee."

Satisfied with his answers, Shelby sat up on the blanket and reached into her basket one final time. She handed Christian a fried peach pie she'd made from her grandmother's recipe.

"You're a good man, Christian, and I believe good things will come to you. Now, let's eat this pie and get out of here. My mosquito repellant is wearing off."

Christian didn't know how to take Shelby's reaction. He couldn't tell if she was bothered by the extent to which he had gone with Alexia or not. He was glad he had gotten the truth out. He did not want to have skeletons popping out later if their relationship progressed. He decided to let it go for now and enjoy the sweet, buttery, pastry that was in front of him.

Shelby watched as Christian consumed the pie. She

didn't know how to feel about the things he had revealed to her. Knowing that he had proposed and been left at the altar by another woman was a lot to take in. She didn't want to be a rebound woman, and she refused to live in another woman's shadow. Shelby was determined to learn more about Christian's relationship with Alexia. Somehow she would also find out what happened to the car and condo.

Chapter Eighteen

Christian walked the length of the building project with blueprints in hand. He and the building foreman inspected the beams and other structural elements as they walked through. Christian visualized the completion of the youth center as his eyes scanned the site. He was pleased with the progress of the center. Everything was on schedule and moving along as expected.

"How are things going?" A man yelled in the distance.

Turning to identify the owner of the voice, Christian waved his hand acknowledging Thaddeus.

With quick steps, Thaddeus joined Christian and the project foreman. Placing his hands on his side he scanned the area. "Looks like things are coming together pretty good."

Nodding his head in agreement Christian replied, "They are. I'm very pleased with the progress."

"That's great," Thaddeus replied. "What kind of time frame are we looking at for completion?"

"Barring any unforeseen weather issues, I estimate we should be finished in twelve to sixteen weeks. Once we get in the dry, the interior will progress rather quickly. The exterior brickwork is a pretty intense process."

"I can imagine it is pretty intense. This is going to be a huge center."

Thaddeus and Christian turned and walked back

towards the mobile office. He looked at his watch and noted the time. He pretended to act surprised even though his plan all along was to catch Christian at lunchtime. Thaddeus wasn't sure what the relationship between Christian and Shelby was but he was determined to find out.

"Wow, I didn't realize it was lunchtime already." Thaddeus stated in mock surprise. "Do you have any plans for lunch?" He asked.

"No, I can't say that I have any plans. Most days I work right through lunch."

"Tell you what, since you don't have any plans why don't I take you to lunch. You know skipping meals really isn't good for you."

Christian eyed Thaddeus suspiciously. He did not know what was going through his mind, but he had an uncomfortable feeling. He decided to have lunch with him, but he would keep his guard up.

"Okay, sure. Let me put these blueprints up and we can go. I hope you don't mind; I'm going to trail you to the restaurant. I need to make a few stops after lunch."

"No problem," Thaddeus declared smiling. "You go ahead and put your stuff up, and I'll wait for you by the car."

The restaurant was a short distance from the job site.

Christian mulled over ideas concerning lunch with Thaddeus. It wasn't like they were friends. In fact, they had only spoken a few times. Now, he was asking him to go to lunch. It just didn't add up.

Christian had to be honest with himself. He had some questions of his own concerning Thaddeus. However, he did not feel like this was the time or the place to address them.

The two arrived at the restaurant and took a seat in a booth. Laneise approached the table.

"Hi guys, how are y'all doing today?"

Christian spoke up first. "Hi, Laneise. What are you doing here this early? I'm used to you working the evening shift."

"Yeah, I know. I've got some unexpected expenses that I have to cover. In order to get it done I needed some extra hours, so I volunteered to work the lunch shift a few days a week."

"I'm sorry to hear that. I hope things get better for you."

"I'm sure they will. Thank you." Laneise offered him a smile and nodded her head. "What can I get you guys today?"

Christian did not have to look at the menu. He had practically memorized its offerings. "I'm in the mood for a burger. I guess I'll have a bacon cheeseburger with grilled onions, fries and a Coke."

Laneise turned to Thaddeus, "And what about you, Sir? What would you like?"

Thaddeus studied the menu intently. "Everything on here looks really good. I guess I'm going to go with the chicken fried steak with white gravy and mashed potatoes. I'll take a sweet tea to drink."

"Okay, I'll get these orders put in for ya, and I'll be right back with your drinks."

Laneise stepped away from the table and left Christian and Thaddeus in awkward silence. Christian turned his attention to the television hanging above the bar.

"I appreciate your joining me for lunch," Thaddeus said hoping to gain Christian's attention.

"No problem, man. Thanks for inviting me."

Laneise walked over with a tray of drinks, and placed their requested beverages in front of each of them. She stepped away quickly delivering the remaining drinks to the table behind them.

"I can imagine it's rather difficult being so far away from home. Especially, with you not having any family or friends here."

"Yeah, but you know, it's all a part of the job. I've dealt with it before." Christian remained cordial but reserved. He felt like Thaddeus was leading up to something, but he didn't want to make any assumptions.

Laneise returned to the table and delivered their meals. Thaddeus waited until after she walked away to continue his line of questioning.

"So what are you doing with your time when you're not working? I mean I know there's not a lot to do around here. Are you making any friends?"

"I've made a few," Christian replied curtly.

Thaddeus ignored his tone. He was going to find out the depth of Christian's relationship with Shelby if it was the last thing he did.

Christian concentrated on his meal. He was beginning to regret accepting the lunch invitation. Had he known his lunch hour would turn into a full-blown interrogation, he would have passed on the offer.

"We need to hang out sometime, Christian. I can show you a few spots that are pretty cool."

"Oh yeah?" Was Christian's only response.

"Yeah, man. I know you like to walk on the wild side."

"What's that supposed to mean?" Christian asked looking Thaddeus directly in the eye.

Raising his hands in surrender Thaddeus said, "Calm

down, man. I'm just messing with you. I mean I tried to warn you about Shelby when you first got here, but I see my warning fell on deaf ears. I won't lie, I was somewhat surprised to see you two at the movies together. Are you dating or something?"

"Look, man, I appreciate lunch and everything, but I'm just going to go ahead and tell you straight up, my personal life is my business. I realize the two of you have some kind of history, but it's not my place to get into all of that."

Christian raised his hand to get Laneise's attention. He asked her for the check and removed several bills from his wallet.

"Look, Christian, I know you're your own man. I can respect that. Shelby is a beautiful woman, and it's only natural that someone that doesn't know her would test the waters. What you said was right. She and I do have history, some good some bad. Have your fun, I'm not trying to stop you. Before you try getting into anything serious though, know that you've been warned."

Christian tossed the folded up bills on the table. "I need to get back to work." He stood to leave. Pausing, he gave Thaddeus a parting shot. "I appreciate your concern. However, I form my own opinions."

Thaddeus raised his glass to Christian, "Touché."

Christian waved goodbye to Laneise, and thanked her for her service. He walked the short distance to his car and climbed inside.

Pulling out of the parking lot, he fumed. Who did Thaddeus think he was? If he kept pressing the issue he was going to see a side of him that he was not ready for. Christian recognized everyone was entitled to their own opinion, but it was his right to reject that view. He and

Shelby had a good thing going and he was determined to see where it would lead them.

Shifting his focus back towards work, he grabbed his cell phone and called Deborah to check in. His lunch with Thaddeus had lasted longer than he anticipated.

Deborah recognized Christian's phone number on the caller ID. She answered the call cheerfully. "What's going on, Christian? What can I do for you?"

"Hey, Deborah, lunch ran a little longer than I anticipated. I need to run a couple errands, and then I'll be back. Did I have any calls, or any pressing matters I need to tend to?"

"Nope, everything is as smooth as silk."

"Sounds good. I'll see you in a little while."

❀ ❀ ❀ ❀

Shelby pulled up the internet search engine and typed in fashion design schools in New York and Los Angeles. Several options pulled up. She looked up the fields of study that interested her. Visual Merchandising Director, Design Director, and Stylist were her top three. She examined the criteria for each. After careful consideration, she decided on stylist.

Her love for fashion influenced her decision. Making people look good was her passion. Shelby reflected on her history in fashion. As a teenager she used her sisters for practice. She laughed at the thought of sneaking into her mother's room while she was at work and borrowing her wigs. She would put wigs on each sister and style multiple outfits for them to model. Sheena would always complain about the outfits she picked for her. Shanelle and Shaunice didn't care. They were happy to be models.

Shelby regretted not pursuing a career in the fashion

industry immediately following high school. Although she would never admit it openly she held a measure of resentment in her heart towards her mother. She wondered if her mother could have done more to save her marriage with their father. With her mother being single it was left up to Shelby to look after her sisters. The ten-year age difference between her and her youngest sister pushed her further behind. By the time they got old enough to fend for themselves, Shelby figured her window of opportunity had closed.

With each passing year, Shelby saw her dream slipping further and further away. She had almost given up until she met Christian. Her life had become so routine that she didn't focus on what she wanted anymore. She jumped on the hamster wheel and settled. Being around Christian made her want to dream again. It was time for her to leave Bethany behind.

Chapter Nineteen

From critically acclaimed playwright Shelia Walton comes the hit stage play I Did it for Love. With odds stacked against her, a woman is in for the fight of her life. Original musical scores and an all-star cast brings passion and intrigue to the Memphis Orpheum Theater. Tickets are selling out fast. Reserve your seats now.

Christian's eyes lit up when the commercial flashed across the screen. He was thrilled. He enjoyed the theater and this play would give him an opportunity to do something with Shelby other than dinner and a movie. Back in Los Angeles, he attended plays and concerts on a regular basis. Alexia didn't share his passion, so he often took members of his staff to the theater with him.

He hoped Shelby would be interested.

On a whim he pulled up the internet and purchased two tickets. If it turned out that she didn't want to go, he would offer the tickets to Daniel and Deborah as a gift. Either way the money would not go to waste.

Grabbing the remote, he muted the television and called Shelby. He tapped on the couch creating a soft drum beat while he waited for her to pick up.

"How did you know I was thinking about you?" Shelby asked with a giggle.

"I didn't know, but now that I do I must say it feels good." Christian replied teasingly.

"Oh it feels good, huh? I like the sound of that. What's going on with you today?"

"Nothing much. I was sitting here watching television, and I saw an advertisement for a stage play at the Orpheum. I was wondering if you would be interested in going with me."

Shelby squealed. "I love plays. In fact, there is one I've been hoping comes to Memphis. I believe it was written by Shelia Walton."

"Oh really." Christian lowered his voice increasing the base tone of it. "What would you say if I told you I just got us front row seats?"

"I would say don't play with me like that. You better not be joking."

"I wouldn't joke about something like that. So what do you say, do you want to go?"

"I absolutely want to go." Shelby squealed, "When is it?"

"Next Saturday. The play starts at 8. I figured we'd grab a bite to eat before the show. I heard about a place called Houston's that's supposed to be pretty good."

"Sounds like you have it all planned out. I'm looking forward to it. The food at Houston's is delicious. You won't be disappointed."

Shelby laid back on her couch, and placed her feet on the armrest crossing them at the ankles. She enjoyed her conversations with Christian. He was easy to talk to, and somehow without realizing it he gave her hope.

"So, tell me what's been going on with you since we last talked."

Christian was genuinely interested in Shelby and everything concerning her. He enjoyed hearing about her work experiences, her friends, and her family. He enjoyed her companionship.

"Things are good. My boss has actually been pretty cool lately. I think it has something to do with her new man. I swear when things are good for her on the relationship front, she is super easy to get along with. She walks around smiling all the time, bringing doughnuts to work. Most importantly she's not breathing down my neck."

"That's what a good man will do for you," Christian interjected.

"I guess. I'm glad somebody defrosted that icy heart of hers. It really makes a difference when I'm working with my customers. She's not looking over my shoulder, and second-guessing everything I do. It gives me the freedom to be creative if you know what I mean."

"I can imagine it does. I suppose that's one of the main reasons I wanted my own business. I believe I'm more of a leader than a follower. That's not to belittle anyone by any means, I just feel some people are born leaders. If I may be frank with you, I believe you're one of those people also. You're the type of person that should have your own business."

Shelby pondered on Christian's words. Did he really see her as a leader? Then again, why would he lie? His statement was confirmation that she was moving in the right direction.

"It's funny you would say that," she said. "I actually have been doing some research on design schools. I'm ready to get out of Bethany. It's about time I move forward with my dreams."

"Is that so? I'm proud of you." Christian stated. "I feel everyone should have the opportunity to follow their dreams. You deserve to be happy, Shelby."

"I can't take all the credit. Christian, you've been a good influence on me. Spending time with you has awakened something within me. When I'm with you, I realize there's more to life than Bethany."

"I don't know what to say to that. I can tell you, you're not alone in your feelings. I feel the same way about you. I genuinely enjoy spending time with you."

Shelby took a moment to process Christian's words to her. She didn't want to assume anything so she chose to remain silent. She felt in her heart it was best to take things moment by moment. The last thing she needed was to be disappointed by the man she felt herself falling for.

"I guess I can use our date as an excuse to go shopping. I need to get cute for the play."

"I'm sure you won't have a problem putting something together. You always look beautiful, even in shorts and a t-shirt."

"Aww, you flatter me. Watch out, Christian, a girl could get used to this."

"As you should, my dear. As you should."

Shelby's phone beeped interrupting their conversation. She pulled the phone from her ear and saw Kim's phone number displayed across the screen. She ignored the call and continued her conversation with Christian.

The phone beeped again. Kim was calling a second time. "That's odd." Shelby said.

"What's odd?" Christian asked.

"My friend Kim keeps beeping in. Normally if I don't answer her call, she'll leave a voicemail or send me a text. She never calls back to back."

"You should probably answer her call. It may be

important. We'll talk soon."

Shelby pressed the button to switch between calls. Kim's breathing was erratic. Panic coursed through Shelby's veins.

"Kim, girl what's wrong with you?" she asked.

"I-I don't know where Julian is." Kim's words were choppy and barely audible. "He's usually home by now. I don't know what to do."

Shelby could feel her heart rate elevating. She struggled to remain calm so that she wouldn't upset her friend any more than she already was.

"Try to calm down, Kim. I'm sure he's fine. Everything will be okay." Shelby offered her words she wasn't sure if she believed herself. "When was the last time you spoke with him?"

"This morning before work. We got into a stupid argument over nothing, so I didn't even kiss him goodbye. I'm so scared. I think something has happened to him. This is not like him at all."

"Did you try calling him?"

"Yes I tried calling him, I've called a hundred times. His phone keeps going straight to voicemail. This is crazy. What if something bad has happened? I can't believe this is happening right now."

The clock on the wall displayed 10:28. Most things in Bethany were already closed and Shelby knew Julian was usually home from work by six o'clock. She didn't want to make any assumptions.

"What can I do to help?"

"Will you come over and stay with the kids? I'm going to go look for him."

"Yeah, I can come over. But Kim, you know it's midnight

black outside, we only have a handful of street lights. You won't be able to see very much."

"Will you just do what I asked, Shelby! I have to find Julian," Kim screamed.

"Kim, please try to relax. I'm sure everything is going to be alright. I'm on my way."

Kim sobbed audibly on the other end of the phone. "Thank you, Shelby. I don't know what I'll do if something has happened to my husband."

"Don't think like that, Kim. He'll be fine I know he will. Try to calm down. The kids don't need to see you all upset like that. I'll be there as soon as I can."

Shelby disconnected the call.

She scrambled around the house gathering her keys, purse, and shoes. She ran out the door, but stopped short when she realized she had forgotten her cell phone.

Shelby darted back inside quickly, grabbed her phone and ran to her car.

Her hands shook as she put the key in the ignition. Hearing Kim so upset had gotten to her. How would she comfort her friend if something bad really had happened? Shelby struggled to push the negative thoughts from her mind. She had to be strong for Kim and the children. She was sure they would ask her questions when they saw her come over and their mother leave suddenly. Shelby rehearsed different excuses to offer the children in hopes of finding one they would believe.

The closer she got to Kim's house, the more nervous she became. Her heart thumped so hard, she could hear the beat ringing in her ears. She turned on Kim's street and her fear immediately turned to confusion. Julian's car sat in the driveway in its normal spot.

"What in the world is going on?"

Shelby parked her car on the street and approached the house. Out of curiosity she walked over to Julian's car and laid her hand on the hood. The heat from the engine warmed her fingers. It was obvious the car had recently been driven. Walking up to the front door she rang the doorbell.

Kim answered the door with red swollen eyes. Her face had salty white lines revealing the path her tears had traveled. Shelby didn't know what to expect.

"I'm sorry, Shelby. It looks like I had you to come all the way over here for nothing. Julian got home a couple minutes ago. I didn't have time to call you, I apologize." Kim's tone was low and shaky.

She stretched her arms and pulled Shelby into an embrace. "Thank you for being willing to drop everything to come and help me. You really are a good friend, Shelby."

"That's what best friends are for. Is everything okay? Is Julian okay?"

Kim rolled her eyes in disgust. "He's fine. He said he was working late. When I asked him why I couldn't get him on the phone he said it was because his phone died and his car charger wasn't working."

Shelby glared at her friend. "Do you believe that? Do you think he's telling you the truth?" she asked.

Kim shrugged her shoulders. "I don't know, I guess. I mean, he's never given me a reason to not trust him. For his sake, I hope he's not lying to me."

Julian approached the door and stood behind Kim. He looked at Shelby and smiled. "Hey Shelby, I take it my lovely wife called you over here."

She gave Julian a hard stare. He was much too jolly

for a man who had upset his wife to the extent that he had Kim. "Yes, as a matter of fact she did. You had my girl worried out of her mind. Not cool Julian, not cool."

"I just heard it from my wife, Shelby. I don't need to hear it from you, too. As you can see, I'm home safe and sound," he snapped.

Shelby did not appreciate his tone. Kim had every right to be upset and his nonchalant attitude was making her even more upset.

"You know what, Kim, since everything over here seems to be back to normal, I'm going back home. I'll check with you later."

Kim nodded her response.

Shelby hopped in her car and sped off. Although she didn't know the full story, with the small piece of information she had received from Kim, and Julian's attitude about the situation Shelby knew something was not right. She planned to find out the truth of what Julian had really been doing.

Chapter Twenty

Christian sat at his desk and tapped his foot to the jazzy beats escaping the small office radio. He flipped through a stack of documents requiring his signature that Deborah had given him. Once he had completed the necessary task, he opened his email and read through the pressing matters.

He was happy to see the email from the ticketing agency containing their tickets for the play. Christian was looking forward to having a date with Shelby that involved more than the usual dinner and movie. Rural Tennessee proved to be very limited in the area of entertainment. Unless there was an annual event or festival going on, their options were few.

Opening his internet browser, Christian typed Houston's Restaurant into the search engine. He clicked on the location he desired and selected the reservation link. Once he completed the reservation process he leaned back in his chair and placed his hands behind his head. He had almost forgotten where he was until Deborah walked up to his desk and cleared her throat.

"So you know this is a small town, right?" she asked with a smirk on her face.

Christian sat up straight in his chair.

"Yeah, so." He replied defiantly.

Deborah raised her hands in surrender. "Relax, it's not like that. Trust me."

Christian felt bad about being so defensive towards Deborah. She clearly meant no harm. His lunch with Thaddeus still had him on edge. Christian was enjoying the relationship he was developing with Shelby and he refused to let anyone or anything hinder it.

"I'm sorry, Deborah. Please, go on with what you were saying."

Deborah looked unsure. She didn't know if Christian would receive her remarks as intended, or if he would become defensive once again. She offered him a tight lipped smile.

Christian sensed her hesitation. He wanted to make her comfortable enough to express herself freely. He decided to give her a nudge.

"Come on, Deborah. What's on your mind?"

Realizing he was not going to let up, Deborah spoke up.

"Well, I was going to say you look happy these days. I heard you've been seeing Shelby Lamar."

Christian braced himself for Deborah's next statement. If Shelby really had the reputation Thaddeus claimed she had, then Deborah was sure to mention it.

"Yes, as a matter of fact I am." Christian pasted on a fake smile.

"I think it's great. Shelby is a nice girl. She's had to deal with a lot, but I feel like she has handled it well."

Christian eyed Deborah suspiciously. "Why do I feel like you're giving a little, and holding back a lot."

"Like I said before. This is a small town. My pastor's wife, Sister Green once told me to eat the fish and spit out the bones."

Christian's forehead wrinkled. He was trying to figure out Deborah's analogy.

Deborah laughed at his expression. She figured the city boy had never heard a statement like that.

"Let me help you out. Basically she was saying when you take in something you have to consider what you consume. Some of it will be useful and some of it you should immediately discard. In other words, don't believe everything you hear. Consider the source."

He had a feeling she was referring to the things Thaddeus had shared with him. He wanted to press her for more information, but she offered him a smile and headed back to her desk.

Christian turned his focus back to his computer screen. Deborah had given him a lot to consider. He felt he was at a disadvantage being from Los Angeles. The local residents always seemed guarded when it came to certain events. He was trying to respect Shelby's privacy, but it was becoming increasingly harder.

Surrendering his heart to another woman was difficult for Christian. He didn't want to get hurt again. He loved the way he felt when he was with her. Simply thinking about her smile lifted his spirits. The more time they spent together, the closer they were becoming. Christian struggled with thoughts of the future. He didn't want to jump the gun because he still was unsure of her feelings towards him.

Christian's cell phone started vibrating on the desk. He picked it up to see who was calling. He immediately recognized the phone number to his corporate office in Los Angeles, which meant it had to be Shantrice calling. Without hesitation he answered the call.

"What's going on?" He asked cheerfully. He was ecstatic to have a call from home.

"Hi, Christian. Everything is good here, how are things on your end?"

Christian stood up and walked away from his desk. He continued outside heading towards the building site.

"Things are going well here. The project is progressing more quickly than we anticipated. The good Lord has blessed us with some awesome weather. At this rate, the center will be finished ahead of schedule."

"That's great. We miss you around here. Everything is running smoothly, but it's not the same without you."

"I miss you guys too. I'm looking forward to getting started on the production studio. I believe when we complete that deal it will open up all kinds of doors for us."

Christian could hear Shantrice shuffling papers on the other end. Following a brief pause, she returned her attention to the call.

"Actually, that's why I'm calling you. I received another letter from Rising Star Studios. They want you to meet with them face to face to sign the contracts. I called them and explained you were currently working on a project in Tennessee. I'm sorry to say it didn't do any good. They were adamant about you attending the meeting."

"Oh, I see."

Christian kicked a rock that was laying by his foot. He looked across the lot at the building project. The exterior was close to completion. This would be a good time for him to get away for a brief moment, to check in at home, and recharge.

"That's not a problem. Have you set the meeting date yet?" He asked, sounding a little more cheerful than he had planned.

"The meeting is set for this coming Tuesday at 10 a.m. I can reschedule it if you need a more convenient time."

Christian was happy the meeting wouldn't interfere with his date with Shelby. With the meeting set for Tuesday he would have Monday to take care of any pressing issues in Los Angeles.

"Tuesday is perfect. Go ahead and book my flight for Sunday morning. I need you to make my return trip back here on Wednesday."

"Not a problem, I'll take care of it right away, Sir."

"Thanks Shantrice. Oh, I almost forgot. Please book me for business class or first class. I want to avoid small children in flight as much as possible."

Shantrice didn't try to hide her laughter. "I tried to warn you when you insisted on flying coach last time."

"Yes, Shantrice you were right. There's no need to rub it in."

She continued to laugh.

"I'll get those flights booked right away. I'll email you the itinerary when I finish."

"Sounds good. Take care and I'll see you next week."

Chapter Twenty-One

Shelby wanted to be excited about her upcoming date with Christian, but her mind was all over the place. Out of all the men she had dated in the past, he was the most genuine. She knew he wanted to make her happy. If she were to be honest, she'd admit she wanted the same for him.

A courier arrived with the boutique's weekly shipment. Following Shelby's lead he placed the large boxes in the storage room at the back of the store. Flashing a brilliant smile, he handed her the electronic tablet to sign.

"What's wrong with you today, gorgeous?" He asked.

With furrowed eyebrows, she softly replied. "There's nothing wrong with me. What makes you ask?"

Hunching his shoulders, he watched her for a few seconds. "I don't know. You look a little tired. You don't have that usual glow about yourself. Plus, your smile looks like someone battling with constipation."

Pushing the tablet towards him, Shelby rolled her eyes. "Shut up Jim. I do not look like that. You better be glad I like you, otherwise I would deck you."

"Yeah, okay. Don't get mad at me because I'm willing to say what everyone is thinking." He teased.

"I guess I am a little tired. Besides, I have a lot on my mind."

Jim's tone changed from teasing to concerned. "It looks like I have successfully put my foot in my mouth again. I'm sorry, Shelby. I hope things work out for you."

"Thank you, Jim. I appreciate that.

Jim looked at his watch, and then back up at Shelby. "I better get back to my route. I've got a full truck today."

Shelby said goodbye to Jim and headed back to the storage room. She desperately needed a distraction. Things were going well between her and Christian, but she was beginning to wonder if they were going too well. She had always done a good job of guarding her heart, but Christian was quickly and quite easily tearing down the wall she had built.

Picking up a small utility knife off the metal counter, she cut the tape on the first box. She was careful not to damage the merchandise contained inside. Returning the knife to the counter, she pulled a stack of crystal embellished blouses from the first box. She carefully examined each garment before placing them on hangers.

Moving on to the next box, her mind drifted over to her best friend Kim. They hadn't spoken since Kim thought her husband was missing. Kim's actions on that night didn't sit well with Shelby. The way Julian reacted to the situation made her believe there was a lot more to the story than what he conveyed. Something wasn't right between those two and she was determined to get to the bottom of it.

Shelby rolled the rack she had placed the new arrivals on out to the sales floor. She moved to the area she had previously prepared for the new merchandise, and busied herself with the task at hand. She was so focused on what she was doing, that she didn't notice the man that entered the boutique.

"Excuse me, Ma'am."

She turned to find Thaddeus standing behind her with a wicked grin on his face. Shelby made no effort to hide the irritation on her face.

"What do you want, Thaddeus?"

"Is that how you treat all of your customers? It seems awful unprofessional of you."

Shelby stepped closer to him. In a hushed tone between clutched teeth she spoke sternly. "We both know you are not in here to make a purchase. After all it's a women's boutique. You came to annoy me."

"How do you know I didn't come to make a purchase. It's not nice to assume."

Shelby smoothed her skirt and pasted on a fake smile. "Okay fine, how may I assist you."

"I need something sexy for a woman I'm going to surprise."

Turning up her lip, she asked, "Something like what?"

"A dress. Make sure it's super short, and very revealing."

Sighing in frustration Shelby asked, "How tall is she?"

"Your height."

"Umm hmm. What size does she wear?"

"Your size," he answered with a smirk.

Shelby had run completely out of patience with Thaddeus. She exhaled roughly.

"Look, I don't have time to play these games with you. I have work to do, and you are wasting my time."

She turned to walk away.

Thaddeus grabbed her arm and turned her towards him.

"Get your hands off me." She exclaimed snatching her arm from his grip. She was glad the store was fairly empty.

She didn't want to disturb the other patrons.

"What is your problem?" Thaddeus replied angrily.

His pale skin had turned crimson. His eyebrows nearly touched, and his ocean blue eyes squinted into thin slits.

"You act like I'm trying to hurt you or something. I came here to offer to take you to lunch. I wanted to give you some information that I think will be beneficial to you. I didn't want you to be blindsided, but you know what I don't care anymore."

"What are you talking about, Thaddeus?" she asked, rolling her eyes.

"I'm talking about your little boyfriend."

Shelby paused. Her breathing was labored. Anger spewed from her lips like venom.

"Why should I believe anything you say. You're a liar and a troublemaker."

"Oh, so you already know he's going back to California in a few days."

Shelby felt like she had been kicked in the stomach.

"Thaddeus don't play games with me. You would do and say anything to get under my skin."

Shelby walked away and began straightening the racks of clothing. There was no way Christian would be leaving without mentioning it to her. As far as she was concerned Thaddeus was stirring up trouble as usual.

Realizing Shelby was not going to talk to him, Thaddeus turned and walked towards the exit. Turning back, he threw one last dagger at her.

"You're going to feel like a fool when you realize I'm telling you the truth."

With that, he made his exit, leaving Shelby seething.

Chapter Twenty-Two

Christian pulled his suit jacket over his shoulders and stepped back to get a full view of himself in the mirror. He was pleased with his selection of a slate blue suit, and navy blue shoes. He chose to leave his pale gray shirt opened at the top. He added white gold, diamond cufflinks to his shirt sleeves. Stepping closer to the mirror he ran his hands over his embedded waves, and splashed on some Gucci Guilty cologne.

He had been looking forward to this night all week long. It was his opportunity to bring two things he truly enjoyed together. He could hardly wait to see Shelby. He placed his wallet in his back pocket, grabbed his phone and keys, and headed out the door.

Looking at the car, he was pleased with his decision to have it detailed. The shine from the wax made it look like a car fresh from the showroom floor. He wanted everything to be perfect. He hopped inside and drove the short distance to Shelby's house. Christian tuned the radio to V101 and tapped his hands on the steering wheel in unison with the old school Rhythm and Blues songs.

Pulling into the driveway his heartbeat quickened. He didn't know what it was about Shelby Lamar, but she awakened emotions in him that he thought were dead and buried. Every fiber of his being wanted to be with her. He desperately wanted to throw caution to the wind and give her his all, but he knew he couldn't.

Shelby scurried around the house applying the finishing touches to her look. She stepped into a pair of black patent leather stilettos with a chrome heel. The shoes perfectly accented her short black plunging neckline dress. The back of the dress boasted an open design revealing her toned back. She finished off her look with teardrop diamond earrings and an open heart diamond necklace.

The doorbell rang notifying her of Christian's arrival. Pushing back thoughts of her conversation with Thaddeus, she glanced at the mirror on her way to the door. Soft waves cascaded down past her shoulders and back. She folded a sheer black shawl and placed it over her arm. Lastly, she placed her cellphone and keys inside a small black clutch.

She opened the door with a warm smile greeting Christian.

"Wow, sweetheart you are so beautiful. It's a good thing we have reservations and have to leave. Otherwise I would have to step inside and examine your ensemble a little closer."

Shelby smiled seductively as he pulled her into a warm embrace. The intoxicating scent of his cologne made her want to lay in his arms all night.

"Look at you, that suit looks like it was made for you."

"It is tailor made. You have a good eye for fashion." Christian extended his arm to her and escorted her to the car.

"It's what I do. I can't help it. Fashion is in my bones."

Opening the car door for her, Christian waited until she was seated comfortably before pushing her door closed and stepping around to the driver's side. He backed out of the driveway and pulled out onto the street. Reaching over to the passengers' seat, he grabbed Shelby's hand and gently kissed the back.

"I hope you're hungry. I made reservations for us at Houston's."

"Good choice, Christian. The food there is delicious."

"I'm glad you approve."

Christian turned onto Main Street and headed for I-40. He made small talk as he drove.

Shelby sat quietly. She joined in the conversation when warranted but she couldn't hide her distance. Christian had seemingly talked about everything except returning home to Los Angeles. She didn't want to prompt him so she patiently waited for him to bring it up.

Christian noticed Shelby was quieter than usual. He didn't want to believe there was trouble between them, so he made it a point to stick with safe topics of conversation. He hoped whatever was bothering her would subside during dinner.

Pulling into the crowded parking lot at Houston's, he parked in the first available spot. He stepped out of the car and straightened his suit jacket before opening the door for Shelby. Placing his hand in the small of her exposed back, he gave her a sensual kiss on the neck.

Shelby giggled at Christian's display of affection. He definitely knew what spot to touch to break her resistance. Maybe Thaddeus was lying. She didn't know why she was giving credit to anything he said any way.

Moving closer to Christian, she released her insecurities and embraced the evening with her man.

Christian pulled on the dark wood and glass door and stepped aside for Shelby to enter. He looked around, admiring the exposed brick and mahogany interior. With Shelby at his side, they approached the hostess stand.

A petite blonde haired woman wearing a black vest and white blouse greeted them with a smile. "Good evening, welcome to Houston's. How may I help you?"

"Good evening. We have a reservation for two please. The name is Christian Tyler."

"Yes Sir, Mr. Tyler right this way.

The hostess escorted Christian and Shelby to a booth. Christian stood until Shelby was seated, before taking his seat. The hostess placed the menus on the table and quietly stepped away allowing their server to take over.

A young man that appeared to be in his early twenties approached the table carrying a pitcher of water and two glasses. He placed the glasses on the table and filled each one. He took extra care to prevent a spill.

"Welcome to Houston's my name is Jesse. I will be your server for this evening. May I start you off with an appetizer or cocktail?"

Christian spoke up right away. "I'll pass on both. Please give the lady whatever her heart desires."

"I'll have a glass of Pascal Jolivet, please."

"Yes, Ma'am. I'll have that for you in just a moment. Are you all ready to order now, or do you need a few more minutes?"

This time Shelby spoke up. "I would like the Scottish Salmon, please."

"Excellent choice." Turning his attention to Christian, he smiled, "And for you, Sir?"

"I believe I'll have the Hawaiian Rib-Eye."

"Ooh, another excellent choice. Chef Gill takes great pride in his steaks. It will practically melt in your mouth.

How would you like that prepared, Sir?"

"Well done, please."

"As you wish, Sir. Let me get these menus out of your way. I'll put your orders in right away."

Looking over at Shelby, he extended a warm smile.

"I'll be back with your Pascal Jolivet, Ma'am."

"I can't believe you're making me drink alone, Christian."

Stretching his hand across the table, he rubbed the back of Shelby's hand.

"I'm sorry, sweetheart. We're pretty far away for home and I prefer driving without any alcohol in my system. As sexy as you are in that dress, I want to make sure I get you home in one piece. I hope you understand."

"Of course I do. Safety first, right."

"Absolutely."

Jesse returned with Shelby's glass of wine and quickly stepped away.

"How are things going at work?" Christian asked making light conversation as they waited for their meals.

"Pretty good, I guess. Not much has changed. My boss still expects a lot, but isn't willing to give up much. I have been after her for a raise for over a year now, but she's still not budging."

"I suppose I can see that from both perspectives. How exactly are you approaching her when you're requesting a raise?"

Shelby let out a soft giggle, "I walked up to her and I say, hey Karen I could really use a raise right now."

Christian laughed. "You have got to be kidding."

"Do you think maybe that's why I haven't gotten it yet?"

"Wow, I can't believe you're serious right now. I would say that's a major part of the holdup. Maybe you should consider a different approach. For instance, you often say she compliments your work. The next time she gives you a compliment, you can use that as your gateway. Say something like Karen, I truly enjoy working here, and I believe I'm an asset. I would like to be considered for a raise."

Shelby nodded her head in agreement. "Man, that sounded pretty good. With your wording I may actually get the raise I want."

"Like I said, I see it from both perspectives. If my employees came to me using both examples, yours and the one I gave I would be more inclined to give the raise to the second person."

"Okay, I'll try it your way. If I still don't get the raise, you will have to cook me dinner. Oh yeah, a foot rub would be good too." Shelby extended her hand to him. "Do we have a deal?"

Christian accepted her hand and shook it lightly. "You've got yourself a deal."

Jesse returned to the table with their meals. "Here you go. Watch out for those plates they're very hot. Enjoy your meals."

Bowing his head, Christian led them in a prayer of thanks.

"Alright baby, let's eat."

Christian cut a thin slice of his steak and placed it in his mouth. He savored the delicious dish. "Mmm, this steak is really good. How's your salmon?" He asked glancing up at Shelby.

Shelby shrugged her shoulders. "It's okay, I guess. Nothing spectacular."

"Really?" Christian was surprised. By all appearances,

Shelby's food looked good.

"Yes really. Here try it for yourself." Shelby pulled off a piece of the fish and offered it to Christian. Leaning in closer, he opened his mouth so that she could feed it to him.

"Maybe I'm overly hungry. It tastes good to me. Would you like to order something different?"

"No it's fine I'll just eat the veggies. I guess I'm not as hungry as I thought I was. Besides, I don't want us to miss the play waiting for them to prepare another dish."

Glancing at his watch, he noted the time. The play was scheduled to start in an hour. He consumed the remnants of his meal over light conversation. Shelby finished a small portion of her meal and drank a few sips of wine. Christian waved at Jesse to get his attention.

"Is everything alright? May I interest the two of you in dessert?"

"No thank you, Jesse. I would like the check please."

"Yes, Sir."

Jesse reached into his apron and pulled out a small black folder. He placed it on the table in front of Christian.

Christian noted the amount and paid the check.

Reaching for Shelby's hand, he pulled her from the bench and kissed her cheek. "Let's go, baby. You are in for a treat."

Chapter Twenty-Three

Kim sat outside Shelby's townhouse with tears streaming down her face. She held Julian's phone in her hand. She was sure he had no idea the phone was in her possession. It was a wonder the phone was still in tact. The screen was a bit scratched, but otherwise it worked fine. Shaking her head in disbelief she scrolled through the pages of text messages.

Hey boo...

What's going on?

Nothing just sitting here missing you with your sexy self

Is that right?

Yes, you left a lasting impression the other night. I can't wait to get some more of that...

What can I say, I aim to please.

Oh you definitely did please I can still smell your cologne in my sheets.

Girl what am I going to do with you.

Hopefully you're going to give me more of what you gave me before.

Oh you want some more huh?

Umm hmm I've never had a man do me like you did me. When are you coming back over? This time I'll take the lead. I'll give you something to make you forget all about that warden you call a wife.

Let me see what I can do.

Here's a sneak peek of what's waiting for you.

Kim threw the phone into the passenger seat. The nude photos of her husband's apparent mistress was too much to bear. How dare he cheat on her. She had been a wonderful wife to him. Her emotions were all over the place. One moment she was angry, wishing she could claw his eyes out. The next minute she was feeling sad, and betrayed.

She used her hands to grip her expanded waist line. She realized she didn't have the same physique she had when they first got married, but she was still the same woman. The woman that vowed to love him unconditionally. The woman that gave birth to his children.

"How could he do this to me!" Kim screamed.

She banged her hands on the steering wheel hoping to relieve some of her frustration. Her eyes burned from the countless tears she'd shed. Her vision was clouded. She knew she couldn't drive in that condition. Climbing out of her car, she walked up to Shelby's front door and knocked.

No answer.

Kim knocked harder. She desperately needed her best friend. She felt bad about shutting Shelby out. The look in Shelby's eyes the last time they saw each other told her she didn't believe a word Julian was saying. Kim couldn't bear the fact that the story Julian gave her that night was a complete lie.

After going through Julian's phone, Kim pulled up his call history. He had calls to the woman throughout the day and immediately after the normal time he left work. The calls stopped for a few hours. Resuming minutes before he arrived home that night. Based on the text messages, she believed that was the time he was with the other woman.

Kim reached for the spare key, but thought better of it. It wouldn't be a good idea for Shelby to come home and find her there unannounced.

❀ ❀ ❀ ❀

"That play was so good!" Shelby exclaimed. Nestling closer into Christian's arms, she wrapped her arm around his waist as they walked to the car.

It had been a long time since she had been to the theater. Even then, it was with Kim and Dominique. She enjoyed the thrill of a live production. Before Christian, no man seemed to share her passions. Everything had always been about what they wanted, or needed to be fulfilled.

The night air had become crisp. Her shawl was no longer providing the warmth that she needed.

Christian noticed her shivering. Being a constant gentleman he pulled off his jacket and placed it on her shoulders.

Shelby looked at him and smiled. "You always seem to know what I need."

"When you have a precious gift, you take care of it."

"Oh so I'm a gift, huh?"

Christian pulled Shelby's face to his and kissed her passionately.

"Let's just say I know what I have."

He opened the car door allowing Shelby to easily slide inside.

Her heart warmed being in Christian's presence. She wanted a future with him. Being with him made her feel like anything was possible. For years, she had been hoping and praying that a man would come along and sweep her off her feet. He would be her own prince charming. They would build a life together. Maybe even raise a family.

"What are you over there thinking about?" Christian asked.

Feeling like a little girl that had been caught playing in her mother's makeup, Shelby gasped.

"What do you mean? I'm just over here chilling."

"Oh, so you always chill with a big ole grin on your face?" Christian teased.

"You need to stop playing. I was not grinning. Besides, how would you be able to see that in a dark car?"

"The light from the dashboard is reflecting off your teeth."

"Yeah right." Shelby reached over and slapped Christian's arm.

The two shared a laugh and engaged in light conversation. Shelby was not ready for the night to end. She wanted to spend every available moment with the man she was growing to love.

Christian reached over and took Shelby by the hand. He gently caressed the back of her hand with his thumb. They were drawing close to the Bethany exit. He knew he would soon have to part ways with his beautiful companion. He still hadn't told her about his upcoming trip to Los Angeles. He was not sure how she would react to it. In his mind, he did not think it would be a big deal, but he learned a long time ago when it came to women, their minds worked differently.

His thoughts drifted to a statement Blake had once made to him when he was having issues with Alexia. Blake's words to him were, "if you give a woman an apple, don't expect a pie because your butt is getting applesauce." Christian laughed inwardly at the thought.

The mood in the car was romantic. He decided to wait until he and Shelby were inside her home to break the news. He turned onto her street and mentally prepared a speech.

"What in the world is she doing here?" Shelby asked aloud.

"Who?" Christian asked in response.

"My best friend, Kim. That's her car in my driveway. I would think she'd be home with her husband and children at this time of night."

Christian pulled into the driveway and turned off the engine. Shelby looked over and noticed Kim laying across the seat.

"Oh my God!" Shelby yelled jumping out of the car.

She knocked frantically on Kim's car window hoping her friend was okay. Kim slowly rose groggily. Her eyes were swollen from crying. She pushed a button to unlock the car door. Shelby immediately pulled on the handle freeing her friend from the car.

Looking up at Shelby, Kim started a new round of sobs and tears."

"Oh Shelby. It's awful." Kim managed to say between sobs.

"Shelby, is there anything I can do to help?" Christian interjected.

She was so distracted with Kim that she had forgotten Christian was with her. This was not the way she expected their date to end.

"I'm so sorry, Christian. "I need to see what's going on with my friend. I hope you understand."

"Of course I do. Hand me your key and I'll unlock the door for you."

Using her freehand Shelby reached into her clutch and handed Christian the key to her home.

Stepping ahead of the women, Christian opened the door and placed the key on the counter. Shelby walked Kim over to the couch, and set her down. She returned to the front door where Christian was standing.

"Thanks for your help. I really do appreciate it."

"No thanks necessary, take care of your friend. We'll talk soon."

Shelby leaned in and gave Christian a gentle kiss on the lips.

"Have a good night. I'll call you as soon as I can."

"You too, sweetheart."

Christian pulled the door closed and walked away. The compassionate side of him hoped Shelby's friend would be okay. However, after seeing Shelby in that dress and reminiscing on the passion they shared throughout the night, the man in him needed a very cold shower.

Chapter Twenty-Four

Shelby turned on the tea kettle and waited for the water to boil. She was both surprised and confused at the same time. She wasn't sure what was going on with her friend, but she knew it was major. In all the years of their friendship she had never seen Kim so distraught. Reaching in the cabinet she pulled out two tea cups and saucers, along with a box of chamomile herbal tea. The tea kettle whistled loudly.

With robotic moves she placed a teabag in each cup, and filled them with the hot liquid. Carefully monitoring her steps, she carried the cups of hot tea into the living room. Kim sat on the couch with the look of exhaustion. Her stringy strands of hair escaped the worn ponytail holder. Trails of black tracks made a path from her eyes to her chin. Makeup filled teardrops littered the front of her shirt.

Shelby sat next to her friend and offered her a cup of tea.

With shaky hands, Kim reached for the cup.

Shelby quickly reconsidered her offer. "You know what on second thought I'm going to sit this down on the table. I would hate for you to get burned. You already look like you've been hit by a Mack truck. What's going on with you, Kim?"

Shelby struggled to lay aside her own anger. She

needed to show her friend compassion. Looking at the condition Kim was in she started to understand why she hadn't heard from her.

Another round of tears flowed from Kim's eyes. She struggled to make complete sentences.

"It-it-it's Julian. Oh God, it's Jul..."

"It's Julian? What about Julian? Is he hurt? Did something happen to him?"

Shelby tried hard to maintain her composure. She didn't want to upset Kim anymore than she already was. But, Kim was going to have to explain herself a little bit better.

"Honey, I understand you're upset, but I don't have a clue what you're trying to tell me."

"Julian is cheating on me," Kim blurted out.

"What!" Shelby exclaimed. "Are you sure, how do you know?"

Kim pulled herself together so that she could give her best friend the details of her husband's affair.

"This morning when he left for work his phone must've falling out of his pocket. I found it in the driveway when I was taking the children to school. He had been acting strange since that night when I called you over to the house. When I found the phone I decided to check things out. Julian is a creature of habit so it wasn't hard to figure out his password. When I unlocked the phone I found messages between him and his mistress. They contained all the gory details. Even after seeing that I still didn't want to believe it. Shelby, I pulled up our phone records. That's when I saw there had been multiple phone calls and text messages between the two." Her voice broke. "I can't believe he would do this to me."

Shelby raised an eyebrow. She wasn't as surprised as Kim was. She had been hit on by enough married men to know the signs. Although Julian had never approached her, the way he behaved towards his wife revealed his lack of interest in her. The last thing Shelby wanted to do was to give her bad advice. She wrapped her arms around her friend and allowed her to cry in her arms.

"Is that why you were spending so much time over here? You know when you were showing up randomly."

Kim looked up at Shelby with tearful eyes. "I was coming over here because he was being so distant and mean to me. Always talking about how I could stand to lose a few pounds. I don't even eat in front of him anymore. That's why I was always eating your food, especially the chips."

"I'm so sorry, Kim. You don't deserve this. You have been faithful to that man since we were in high school." She softened her tone and lifted Kim's head with her hand. "What are you going to do?"

"I don't know. The idiot probably doesn't even realize I know. I called his mother to come over and stay with the children once they got out of school. I told her I had an appointment. She said she would stay with them until he got home. I turned my phone off so that he couldn't contact me. Seeing as though I have his phone I don't guess he'll be contacting her tonight either."

Looking at her friend, sincerely Shelby replied. "I don't think that was a good idea. I'm sure the children are wondering where you are. Even if you are mad at him you shouldn't take it out on the children. Like it or not, Kim you are going to have to deal with this. You're a grown woman, and you are going to have to handle it as such."

"Really Shelby, that's how you're going to come at me.

Honestly, I have been through enough already. I don't need you coming down on me."

"Wait a minute. I am not the enemy. Don't be displacing your anger. I'm just trying to tell you; you have to deal with this. This is serious. It's not only about you and Julian, y'all have a family. You're welcome to stay tonight if you want to. I honestly don't think you should drive as upset as you are. Please call Julian and let him know where you are."

Shelby picked up her cup of tea and consumed it. Once again, she embraced her best friend.

"I love you, Kim. Please know that I'm here for you."

"Fine Shelby. I'll do it your way, but I won't be forced into a decision."

"Girlfriend, I'm not trying to force you into anything. Look it's late, I'm tired, and I'm pretty sure you are too. Call your husband, and then try to get some rest. You know where everything is."

Shelby embraced her friend once again, stood, and walked away. Glancing back over her shoulder, she said, "It's going to work out, Kim. You'll see. We can talk some more in the morning. Get some sleep."

Kim watched as Shelby walked into her bedroom. She rolled her already swollen eyes in defiance. She knew Shelby was right, but this was one time she wished she had been wrong. Pulling her cell phone out of her pocket she pressed the button to turn it on. Her voicemail was full. Most of the messages were from Julian. She deleted them without listening to any of them. In addition to the voicemails, she also had several text messages.

Good for him. Now he sees how I felt the night when I couldn't reach him. She thought. The thought of Julian being with another woman left her enraged. She keyed in the numbers to her home phone and waited for Julian to answer. It was time she gave him a piece of her mind.

Chapter Twenty-Five

Christian tossed a few items in a bag and prepared for his trip home. He looked at his cell phone for what seemed to be the hundredth time. Still no word from Shelby. He hated that he didn't get to tell her about his trip when they were together. He realized her friend needed her. There was no way he would be selfish enough to interfere. He could only hope Shelby wouldn't be upset about finding out about his trip through voice mail.

Making one final attempt, he dialed Shelby's number. Much like several times before the call went straight to voicemail. Unable to wait any longer he tossed his bag in the car and headed for the airport. The thought of returning home brought an immediate smile to his face. He was looking forward to sleeping in his own bed, checking on his mother and his company, and hanging out with his best friend.

He knew the change of environment would do him good. More than anything he looked forward to being away to sort out his thoughts and feelings about Shelby. Being so far away from home in an unknown environment without any friends or family limited the scope of his focus. Other than work, Shelby was pretty much the only other thing he could focus on. Going back home would help him to see if his feelings for her were genuine.

Christian decided to make one final phone call before

hitting the road. He keyed in the number for Daniel Joseph. He wanted to remind him of his trip, and to give him instructions for the crew in his absence. He also wanted to confirm Daniel had all of his contact information. Once he completed his phone call, Christian entered the name of the airport into the navigational system. Having made prior arrangements to leave the car at the airport while he was in California, he wouldn't have to worry about transportation upon his return.

"Sunny California here I come."

❀ ❀ ❀ ❀

Shelby climbed out of bed and stretched. A slight overcast made the day seem gloomy. She didn't realize how tired she was until her head hit the pillow. She felt as if she had slept a full twenty-four hours. Heading into the restroom she completed her morning routine before joining Kim in the living room.

"Good morning, Kim."

She spoke gently, not knowing what Kim's mood would be. Last night was the most upset she had ever seen her friend. Kim was one of those people Shelby referred to as silent sufferers. No matter what she was going through she always bottled everything up until she could no longer contain the contents of her heart.

"Hey Shell. How are you this morning?"

"I'm doing just fine. You're the one I'm concerned about. Did you sleep okay last night?"

"As much as can be expected, I guess."

"What about Julian?"

"What about him?" Kim snapped.

Realizing her tone was harsher than necessary, Kim

recanted. "I'm sorry, Shell. You didn't deserve that. I don't know how he's doing right now. To be perfectly honest, I don't care."

"Did you call him last night?"

"Yeah I called. I had so much I wanted to say to him. Instead I said nothing. I told him that I would be home today, and that I needed to talk to him."

"How did he respond?"

"I have no idea. I hung up the phone and turned my phone off. I didn't want to talk to him last night. I only called because you kept trippin."

Shelby burst into laughter. "No you didn't."

Kim laughed along with her. "Don't be trying to act innocent now. You know you're pushy. Last night you gave me the business. I think it has something to do with that fine man you came home with. Looks like my puffy eyes and snotty nose interrupted something."

Shrugging her shoulders Shelby smiled at her friend.

"I guess we'll never know. Real talk though, your timing was messed up."

"My bad, girl."

Kim stood up from the couch and gathered the blankets she had used. She folded them neatly and return them to the linen closet.

"What time are you planning to head home?" Shelby asked.

"I'm actually getting ready to leave now. I wanted to wait until you were awake first. I need to go and check on my babies. I'm sure they don't know what to think."

Looking on her friend with compassion Shelby replied, "I know they're missing their mama. Kim, don't let the fact that you spent a night away from them get to you. I would rather have you here last night than for you to go home and confront him with them there. This is a very emotional situation. You needed time to cool down."

"Yeah, I guess you're right. I was beyond upset last night. Don't get me wrong, I'm still pissed. Now I feel like I can at least talk about it. Last night all I felt was rage."

"Well honey, please don't go to jail. I can't be having my god babies' mama in the slammer."

Kim couldn't help but to laugh at the expression on Shelby's face. She could imagine Shelby pulling her hair out trying to keep up with all of her children. She could be wrong, but Shelby didn't strike her as the maternal type. Having no sisters of her own, Kim felt Shelby was the logical choice to be her children's godmother.

"Girl, let me get out of here. I have taken up enough of your time. I'm sure that man of yours is wondering why he hasn't heard from you yet."

Kim gathered her purse and turned to Shelby. "Shell, I really hope things work out for you. You deserve to be happy. I'm rooting for you."

"And I'm praying for you, Kim. I love you, girl."

"Me too."

Kim threw her hand up and waved goodbye to Shelby.

Shelby walked into the kitchen and prepared a ham and cheese sandwich. She figured it was too late to fix breakfast. Coffee didn't even sound appealing to her. She poured a glass of lemonade to go along with her sandwich.

She gathered her meal and walked over to the small round table in her dining area. Between bites, she thought about what Kim had said. Seeing the pain her friend was in, the last thing on her mind was a serious relationship. She hoped Kim and Julian would be able to work things out. The last thing she wanted to see was another broken family.

Christian showed such compassion and understanding when they parted ways the previous evening. Maybe he was a keeper.

She snapped her fingers.

Suddenly realizing she hadn't called Christian, she placed her dishes in the kitchen sink and went in search of her phone.

"I'm surprised he hadn't called me," she spoke aloud.

She found her phone inside her clutch on her night stand. The phone was completely dead. In all of the commotion with Kim, she had failed to put the phone on charge. Quickly reaching for the power cord, she plugged the phone up and waited until it had enough juice to power up.

Chapter Twenty-Six

The airport was packed with travelers. Christian was glad he didn't have to check a bag. All he had was his carry-on which contained his electronics. He felt it unnecessary to bring clothes of any sort seeing as though he was going home. Everything he needed was already there at his disposal.

The security checkpoint line seemed to go on forever. He glanced down at his watch to verify the time. He thought he had arrived in plenty of time to catch his 8:55 am flight. Now, judging from the size of the security line he wasn't so sure. He hated the idea of having to run to his gate.

Ten minutes later, he was finally able to go to his gate. He wanted to get a cup of coffee from Starbucks, but decided against it. He couldn't risk missing his flight. He figured he could get something to drink on the plane anyway.

By the time he arrived at the gate the passengers were already starting to line up. He looked around at his traveling companions. Noting the number of small children waiting to board along with their parents he was glad he had decided to fly business class. He didn't want a repeat of his last flight.

The announcement was made for business class passengers to board the plane. Christian quickly approached the agent and presented his boarding pass.

Once he was on board the plane he chose to put his carry-on bag under the seat instead of the overhead compartment.

He pulled out his cell phone and checked for messages from Shelby. She still had not responded to any of his messages. He attributed her lack of response to the time of day. Figuring she wasn't awake yet. He decided to send a quick message.

Hey sweetheart, I'm on the plane. I'll have to turn my phone off soon. I have a pretty full schedule when I get to Los Angeles. I'll check with you when I return.

Christian quickly pressed the Send button before he changed his mind. He didn't want to be overly aggressive with his communications. Especially since he was still trying to figure things out. No matter what, he was determined to not contact Shelby while he was away.

With moments left until takeoff Christian sent a text message to his mother notifying her of his flight number and arrival time. She was thrilled about him coming home. It didn't matter to her that it was only for a couple of days. She had told him on several occasions that she missed him dearly.

Reclining his seat, he closed his eyes and relaxed.

❀ ❀ ❀ ❀

Shelby picked up her phone and checked the battery status.

"Finally," she declared out loud as she pressed the Power button.

Her phone chimed indicating voicemail messages, and text messages. She clicked on Christian's name. Sadness filled her heart when she realized Thaddeus was telling the truth. Christian really did go back to Los Angeles. She took comfort in knowing he would only be gone a few days. However, she didn't understand why he would not be communicating with her while he was gone.

Various scenarios played in her mind concerning the reason for his trip back to California. She wanted to believe it was work related. Part of her wondered if he had a girlfriend or worse a wife that he was going home to be with. She struggled to remain optimistic, but after seeing what Kim was going through she didn't want to let down her guard.

Shelby's phone beeped reminding her of the unheard voicemail messages. She pushed the button hoping there would be one from Christian. Maybe then it would give her solace. On the first message Christian simply said he was checking on her. The second message was a pleading call from Sheena asking her to call her. Without a second thought Shelby deleted Sheena's message. She figured her sister was asking for money again. A question to which she would promptly respond with a resounding no.

The last message on her phone was from Christian. This time he was more detailed. He explained he was leaving town. He told her how long he will be away, and that it was a business trip. Much like his text message, he indicated he would not be communicating with her. He did not, however, reveal the time of his flight. He told her she was welcome to call him prior to him leaving if she got the message in time.

Looking at the clock on the wall, Shelby realized it was too late to call him. The fact that he had left both a text message and voicemail stating he wouldn't contact her while he was away, infuriated her. She didn't understand why he felt the need to stress it. She reasoned within herself that what he was actually saying was that he didn't want to be bothered.

"Fine Christian." She stated as if he could hear her. "If that's the way you want it, then that's the way you'll get it."

Who did he think she was anyway?

She was not the one to sit around and wait for a man to call her. He was in for a rude awakening. The next time they spoke would be after his return, that was for sure. However, it would be on her terms.

Christian Tyler had shown his hand, and she had seen him for who he really was.

Chapter Twenty-Seven

Stepping off the plane, Christian headed for the terminal exit. L.A.X was much busier than the airport in Nashville. He had not reached the street yet, but was already experiencing the change in environment. His adrenaline pumped as he mentally prepared for the Los Angeles traffic. Although he wouldn't be driving, he knew the cabbies were assertive drivers.

Coming off the escalator he had to pass the baggage claim area in order to exit the terminal.

"Yo, Chris," he heard someone yell in the distance.

Looking around to identify the voice, he discovered Blake waving. Christian's lips parted into a wide grin. He was so happy to see his best friend. Stepping quickly, they closed the gap between them and greeted each other with a brotherly hug.

"Man, what are you doing here?" Christian asked beaming with delight.

"What do you mean, what am I doing here? There is no way my boy is coming home and I not be here to greet you."

"Ah, man. I appreciate that, dawg."

Pointing to the bag in Christian's hand Blake asked, "Is that all you got?"

"Yeah this is it. I have everything I need at home already. No sense in bringing any extra weight."

"Okay, cool. Let's go." Blake led him out to his car.

Once they were inside the car, Blake leaned over towards Christian and sniffed.

"Man, what are you doing? I know you ain't flipped on me while I was gone."

"Nah, man. Never that move. I was just checking to see if you came back smelling like cows or something."

"Aw you got jokes, I see."

Blake burst into laughter. "Dawg, I couldn't resist. I have been planning that joke for the longest.

Christian shook his head. "Man, you crazy. Take me home."

Laughing, Blake backed out of his parking spot and left the terminal. He jumped on the 105 and headed towards Christian's house.

"So Blake, what's been going on with you lately?"

"Same ole, same ole. Working hard and playing even harder."

Christian shook his head at his best friend. Based on that response he knew absolutely nothing had changed with him. One thing was for sure Blake was honest. He never made promises to the women that he was involved with that he wasn't willing to keep. Christian had no idea why the women continuously put up with Blake's antics.

"What you got going on tomorrow night, Blake?"

"Nothing really, I knew you were coming in so I figured we could get into something together. Maybe hit the club scene."

"Yeah, we can make that happen." Christian agreed.

Blake accelerated and moved to the far right lane. His exit was approaching and he did not want to miss it.

"You know 1 OAK will be jumping. The chicks that hang

out there are always fine. Now that you're back from the farm you need to get your feet wet."

Christian shook his head. "Man, you *do* realize I'm only in town for a couple of days, right? I'm really not trying to get into all of that."

Pulling in front of Christian's house, Blake moved the gearshift into the Park position and turned off the ignition.

"Chris, man what are you talking about? I can't believe this is you talking to me. Being in the country has slowed you down. I knew you were gone too long."

Laughing at his friend, Christian climbed out of the car. He reached into his bag and took out his house keys.

"I'm serious, I have a lot going on tomorrow."

Blake followed him into the house. He took a seat on the couch. Something didn't add up when it came to Christian. He struggled to figure out what had prompted the change in his best friend. He snapped his finger with the enthusiasm of one that had won a prize.

"It's that chick you've been hanging out with isn't it? Man, she's got your nose wide open. That corn bread booty's got you hooked."

Christian burst into laughter. Blake was a man that said exactly what he was thinking. This time was no different, he did not hold back.

"I keep telling you that we're just friends it's nothing serious between me and Shelby."

"You can say whatever you want to say. Your face is telling a different story. Just the mention of that chick's name and you lit up like the sun."

Plopping down in the seat across from Blake, Christian smoothed his head with his left-hand. As much as he hated to admit it, Blake may be on to something.

"Man, I don't know what's going on. I didn't plan on developing feelings for her, but somehow it happened. She's wearing on me. I asked her to not contact me while I'm in L.A. I figured I could take this time to sort out my feelings."

"I don't know if that was the best idea," Blake stated. "Women are funny like that. You probably have all kind of thoughts going through her mind right now."

"I didn't even think about that. You're probably right."

"Of course I'm right. One thing I know is women. My advice to you, is to be prepared for some drama when you get back to the dirty south."

"I guess we'll see." Christian placed his hands on the arms of the oversized chair he was sitting in and stood to his feet.

Blake stood up to leave. "I know you want to go by and see your mom. I've got a few things I need to take care of myself. Give me a call later and we can plan out a real homecoming for you."

Christian shook his friend's hand, and followed it up with a one armed hug. Alright Blake man, I hear you. Thanks again for picking me up."

"No need for thanks, man. I'm glad I was able to do it."

Walking through his house, Christian surveyed his surroundings. He could tell his mom had been at his home. The plants she had given him stood vibrantly in their pots. The shelves looked freshly dusted. He thumbed through a stack of mail placed neatly on the coffee table. Nothing significant stood out to him. Returning the mail to the table he went into the bedroom and stretched out across the bed.

"Boy, did I miss you."

He spoke to the bed as if it was a person. No matter how far he traveled he always enjoyed coming home. Looking around at his familiar furnishings and accessories for the first time he felt like something was missing. Who was he kidding it wasn't something that was missing it was someone. He felt the pain in his heart as he began to acknowledge his true feelings.

The phone rang rescuing him from his thoughts. He looked at the display and smiled. Words couldn't express how much he truly missed her.

"Hello," he answered with unmistakable enthusiasm.

"Hey, baby. How are you doing?"

"I'm doing great, mom."

"I've missed you so much, son. When are you coming by here? I've already started cooking. I'm marinating some steaks to put on the grill, and I'm making twice baked potatoes. I made a key lime pie and chocolate cake for you earlier today."

"That sounds good. Give me just a little while to take a quick shower, and then I'll head over that way."

"Alright then, give me a call when you're on your way so that I can put the steaks on."

"Okay, I will. See you soon."

Chapter Twenty-Eight

Shelby took quick steps to answer the ringing doorbell. She was happy to finally hear from Kim earlier that morning. Now that she'd had time to cool off, she was willing to talk to Shelby about her and Julian.

Turning the knob, Shelby swung the door open. She pulled Kim into a warm hug.

Kim returned the gesture and followed the familiar path into the living room. Once Kim had taken a seat, Shelby sat on the couch and pulled her feet up.

She looked upon her friend with compassion. Heavy bags had settled below Kim's eyes pulling all of the light out of them. Shelby didn't want to be overly dramatic, but she was sure Kim had added a few gray hairs since she last saw her.

They sat silently for several seconds.

Shelby didn't want to push her, so she waited patiently for Kim to speak.

Kim studied her hands, rubbing her thumb across each nail as if she was testing the polish. She looked up at Shelby like she was trying to figure out what to say. Kim started to speak but then cowered down.

In an effort to ease the tension that had settled in the room, Shelby spoke up. "I'm glad you came by today, Kim. I've been thinking about you a lot. I also sent up a few prayers on your behalf. How are things going?"

"I guess they're going as good as can be expected. That is for someone that just caught her husband cheating and all."

Shelby didn't want to press too hard. She figured she had at least broken the ice, and now their conversation could flow more freely. Deflecting from Julian's infidelity, she changed the subject.

"How are the kids doing? I need to get over there to see my babies." Knowing how much Kim adored her children, Shelby figured the topic would cheer her up.

"They're fine," was Kim's brief response.

Shelby looked at Kim and rolled her eyes. She understood her friend was upset about what happened with her husband, but enough was enough. She had issues of her own to deal with. Kim had brought in a dark cloud so big that Shelby was sure it would start lightning and pouring rain in her living room at any moment.

"What you gone do?" Shelby asked bluntly. She didn't care that her English was broken. A moment like this called for pure Ebonics.

Kim looked at Shelby in surprise. "Really, Shelby? That's how you're going to come at me?"

"I'm just saying, you're my girl, Kim. I can't stand to see you all humdrum like this. You know what you're dealing with. Make a plan of action and move forward with your life. You can't be walking around here looking and feeling all depressed. Pick yourself up. Things will get better."

"That's easy for you to say," Kim uttered. "You're not the one going through it. Since you want to know so bad, I've decided to stay. I've put too many years into this to just let it go. I was the one there when he was working temporary jobs and we were living in the studio apartment.

I'm not about to let some little slut come and destroy all that I've worked so hard to build."

"So you're going to forgive him and pretend nothing ever happened. Just like that?" Shelby snapped her fingers to emphasize her point.

"I'm not saying all of that. Real forgiveness in my opinion takes time. I'm not leaving my home or my marriage, point blank. I've put too much time into building my family to this point. I refuse to allow some tramp to come along and ruin everything that I have."

Shelby looked at her best friend with sincere compassion. "You know what, Kim, if that's what you want to do then I'm all for it. It takes a strong woman to make a decision like that. I admire your courage."

"Don't get me wrong, I know it's not going to be easy. I'm pretty sure there will be days that I'll probably regret my decision. When I said I do, I meant it. Only God knows what the future holds."

"That's for sure," Shelby replied, nodding her head in agreement.

Kim rose from the couch and went into the kitchen. She retrieved two bottles of water from the fridge, and some potato chips from the counter. Returning to the living room she handed Shelby a bottle of water and plopped back down on the couch.

Lightening the mood, Shelby teased. "Make yourself at home, why don't you."

Kim waved her hand in the air dismissing Shelby's sarcasm. Holding the bag out to Shelby, she offered her the salty snack.

"Enough talk about me. Tell me what's going on with you and Christian. I know I was hysterical the other night, but even then I could tell the two of you have some serious chemistry going on."

The tables had been turned, and the spotlight was shining directly on her. There was no way Kim would allow Shelby to slip by without answering her question.

"I really don't know what to say when it comes to me and Christian. I thought things were going extremely well. That is until I received a voicemail message from him, telling me he was returning to California for a few days."

"What's wrong with that?" Kim asked before popping another chip in her mouth.

"Normally, I would say nothing. I'm tripping because he made it a point to repeatedly tell me he would not be contacting me while he was away. He also closed the door to me calling or texting him."

Kim took a gulp of water. "That is kind of strange. If you had told me this last month, I would have said you were overreacting. Now that I'm dealing with this stuff with Julian, I feel differently. All I can say is watch everything, girl. These men are as slick as a wet fish. California is a long way away. A lot can happen between here and there. Follow your gut. Don't ignore your intuition, you'll know if he's legit or not."

Shelby considered her words. The last thing she wanted to do was to jump to conclusions when it came to Christian. At the same time, she was nobody's fool. She thought about a phrase her mom always said to her. *What doesn't come out in the wash, will certainly show up in the rinse.*

Chapter Twenty-Nine

Christian wrapped up dinner with his mother. After filling her in on all things Tennessee, he headed home. His mind drifted to his plans for the following night with his best friend. Typically, he would be excited about hanging out with Blake. One thing was for sure, he could count on having a good time. Somehow this time felt different.

Since meeting Shelby, his focus seemed to shift. He wasn't interested in meeting anyone. Christian had never been the one to indulge in quick thrills like Blake. Unlike his best friend, he had always tried to maintain a level head. He didn't like to admit it, but he had a tendency of becoming emotionally attached.

Looking down at his phone he considered calling Shelby. Rubbing his hand across the face of his phone he thought better of the idea. He was determined to stick to his original plan of not contacting her. This is the only way he would truly know if his feelings for her were genuine.

Christian merged onto the 405 heading towards Brentwood. He never understood why his mother insisted on remaining in Inglewood. He had offered to purchase her a home near him in Brentwood, but she refused to leave her neighborhood. After several failed attempts, he gave up on the idea.

"Home sweet L.A.," he said as he slowed to a halt on

the freeway. No matter the time of day, he could expect a traffic jam on the busy 405. Inching along, his mind easily drifted towards Shelby.

He scanned the vehicles around him and noticed a young woman with the top down on her convertible Mercedes. She drummed on the steering wheel to the beat of a song playing on her radio. Christian imagined Shelby in that setting. He wondered how well she would adapt to the California lifestyle.

"Beep, Beep!"

The sound of a horn blowing behind him caused him to jerk. He raised his hand as a sign of apology to the driver behind him. This was getting out of hand. He needed to focus on something other than Shelby Lamar. He couldn't wait to get home and crash for the night.

※ ※ ※ ※

"Man, are you ready yet? Being in that little town has made you soft. You're moving around here like you're walking through mud."

Blake checked his watch for the time. He wasn't used to this new Christian. He realized now more than ever he had to get his friend back together.

"Come on, man," he urged.

"Man, will you chill out?" Christian replied as he entered the living room.

"It's about time you're ready. You already told me you can't stay out too late. I'm trying to find me a sweet little honey to hook up with tonight."

"Look dawg, I'm not trying to be your wing man tonight."

Blake tapped Christian on his shoulder. "Man relax, it's not even like that."

Christian followed Blake out to his silver Lamborghini and hopped inside.

"I see you pulled out all the stops tonight. I hope you don't expect me to take a taxi home."

Laughing at Christian's comment Blake replied, "You know I wouldn't do you like that. This is your welcome home party, I figured we should ride in style."

Christian sat back against the soft leather seat, and listened to the roar of the engine. Sometimes he wished he was more adventurous like Blake. He had always been the more conservative of the two. Although his business was very lucrative, at times it could appear boring. He always focused on stability. Blake on the other hand, worked in the entertainment industry. His parent's wealth allowed him access that the average person could only dream of.

"Man, you're in deep aren't you?" Blake asked.

"What are you talking about?"

"I'm talking about that chick. I mean it's like you're here, but you're not here."

"I just have a lot on my mind. I'm ready to get this project finished, so I can get back to my life. Being away from home hasn't been as easy as I thought it would be."

"I hear what you're saying, but it's more to it than that. I've known you a long time. You're falling hard for this girl."

"I wouldn't say all that."

Blake turned and looked at his friend. "You don't have to. You're in here screaming with your mouth closed."

"Man, don't you think you're being a little dramatic, Blake?"

Blake raised his hands. "I'm just calling it like I see it. I hope your lovesick behind don't ruin my night."

"Whatever, man."

Christian opened the car door and stepped out onto the curb. He waited for the valet to give Blake a claim ticket. Flashing camera lights practically blinded him, as he and Blake made their way towards the entrance.

"Man the paparazzi is in full force tonight. I wonder who they're chasing."

"It could be anybody. You know how it goes. You haven't been gone that long." Blake replied.

"You're right about that." Christian agreed.

Stepping closer to the entrance, He heard a loud yelp.

"Oh my, gosh, Christian is that you."

Immediately his body began to tense up. Christian had barely been back in the city a full twenty-four hours. What were the chances of him running into Alexia? He cut his eyes at Blake. The entire scene felt like a set up.

Blake raised his palms and shook his head, feigning innocence.

Ignoring Christian, Blake walked into the club leaving him and Alexia behind.

Alexia wrapped her arms around him, and kissed him deeply on the lips. Just as her lips made contact the camera flashed. Placing his arms on her shoulders he pushed her away.

"What are you doing?" he questioned her bitterly.

"What do you mean?" Alexia replied still smiling for the camera.

"I don't know what kind of stunt you are trying to pull. But I know you're up to something." Christian's tone was harsh.

"Why do you always have to be such a prude, Christian? Why can't you just follow along?"

Christian's nostrils began to flare. "I'm not going to ask

you again."

Alexia could tell he was serious. "Where have you been that you don't know what's going on?"

He gave her a stern look.

"Let's just say, I was caught in a very compromising position. With my acting career taking off, I can't afford the bad press. I needed to let the world know I have a man of my own."

"You and I both know I am not your man. You made sure of that a very long time ago."

"Why must you be so bitter? Let it go, Chris. Besides this is Hollywood. In a couple of days, it'll be old news. Let it ride."

"I see you're the same sneaky conniving Alexia. I don't know what you did, but I'm sure one kiss is not going to fix it. You really need to get a life." Christian used the back of his hand to wipe off the sticky gloss Alexia left behind.

"One kiss may not get it, but that kiss along with all of the pictures that we have together will certainly serve its purpose."

Blake stepped outside to find Christian standing on the sidewalk. He noticed Alexia standing beside him. Judging from the expression on Christian's face, he knew it couldn't be good.

"Man, I thought you were inside. What's going on out here?"

Christian stepped away from Alexia, giving her a menacing glare.

"Blake, man, take me home. I've had all I can take tonight. I'm suddenly feeling sick to my stomach."

Blake scanned Alexia hoping for an explanation, but received none.

"Man, I know you aren't going to let this scrub ruin your evening." He turned his nose up at Alexia.

"Who are you calling a scrub?" she shot back.

"I'm sorry, what I meant to say was trash."

"You know what Blake, you can…"

"Don't try me. You know I have the power to destroy the piece of career that you're fighting so hard to have. Walk away while you still can."

Alexia turned and walked away, blowing a kiss at Christian in case the photographers were still looking. He turned his head in the opposite direction.

Turning his attention towards Blake, Christian urged, "Take me home."

Chapter Thirty

Shelby retrieved the mail from the mailbox, and walked towards her house. She flipped through the stack of mail noting the senders.

"Bills, bills, bills," she's sang as she got closer to her front door. She gasped loudly as she stood on the walkway. At the bottom of the stack there was a letter from The Fashion Institute.

She willed herself to go inside, but her feet wouldn't move. Her heart began to pound against her chest. The words contained in that letter could be the key to her fulfilling a lifelong dream.

Tucking the stack of mail under her arm, she gently opened the letter. Her hands shook as she unfolded the ivory colored paper.

Shelby read the letter three times before her feet became unglued from the cement. She jumped up and down causing the rest of her mail to go flying into the air.

Tears of joy formed in her eyes. "I got in. I can't believe it. I actually got in," she cheered aloud while picking up the envelopes from the ground.

Once Shelby had made it inside her home, she laid the letter out on her dining room table. She read the letter once again.

Dear Ms. Lamar,

It is with great pleasure that we welcome you to The

Fashion Institute's student body. The Fashion Institute is an elite institution that is responsible for the careers of the fashion industry's most successful designers and stylist. With campuses in both New York City, New York and Los Angeles, California we will provide you with the tools you need to become Fashions next success. Please logon to our website to complete your registration, and to select the campus of your choice. Your prompt attention to this matter is requested.

Shelby covered her mouth with her hand. It seemed as if she had waited her whole life to receive this letter. Her dreams we're finally coming true.

She grabbed her phone and started to dial Christian's number. Her heart sank as she recalled his message to her concerning no contact.

Not one to be defeated, Shelby dialed her mother's phone number instead.

Linda answered the call after the first ring. Her excitement penetrated the phone line. A smile instantly formed on Shelby's lips. She could tell her mother was in a great mood. Hopefully, her news would add to her mother's excitement.

"Hey, Mama," Shelby squealed into the phone.

"What's going on baby girl? I was just thinking about you."

"Mama, you will not believe what happened to me today. I have literally been jumping up-and-down."

"Well, tell me what it is so I can jump to." Linda replied.

"I got in, Mama. I have wanted this for so long and now I finally have it."

"Shelby, what on earth are you talking about? I may be your mama, but I can't read your mind."

Laughing into the phone, Shelby realized her mother didn't have a clue as to what she was talking about.

"Let me start over. A short while ago, I applied for admission into The Fashion Institute. It is the top school for the fashion industry. Ninety-eight percent of the people that apply to this school are rejected. I on the other hand was accepted."

"Wow, baby that's amazing. You always have had a love for that kind of thing. Where is this school at? Up around Nashville somewhere?"

"That's the thing, they only have two locations in the United States. New York City and Los Angeles."

"You mean to tell me you're thinking about moving that far away from home?"

Linda's voice took on a disappointed tone. Being the oldest daughter, Shelby was the one she could always count on. She didn't want to destroy her daughters dream, but she couldn't imagine her being so far away.

"Yes, Mama. I would have to move there. I haven't decided which location I'll choose yet. I have a few weeks to make my decision. If I'm going to be successful, I have to go where the action is."

"Yeah, I suppose you do. It sure is going to be different around here with you so far away."

"Oh, Mama it's not going to be that bad. I'll visit home often. Who knows you may end up wanting to move there to. This could be a new beginning for all of us."

"Chile, I wouldn't know what to do in a city that big. There's too much going on. All that crime and stuff. I see it on the TV all the time."

Shelby wanted to convince her mother otherwise, but she knew it would be a waste of time. Linda had spent her entire life in and around Bethany. The thought of being in a large city petrified her. Perhaps Shelby could start off with small visits to get her out of her shell. Right now she realized it wasn't a good idea to press the issue.

"Enough about me, Mama. What's going on with you? You were awful perky when you answered the phone. Have you got a new man or something?" Shelby teased.

"Girl please. Ain't nobody thinking about no man. I'm sitting here laughing at these sisters of yours. They were telling me about their track meet. Shaunice said Shanelle was so tired from running, that she laid her head on her shoulder and practically walked the rest of the race. She tried to quit but the coach told her she better keep going."

Linda burst into another round of laughter. Shelby loved to hear her mother laugh. Linda had the kind of laugh that would cause others around her to laugh as well. A trait that she herself also had.

"What kind of race was she running?" Shelby asked joining her mother in laughter.

"Chile, I don't know, but I hate I missed it. It's sounds like it was hilarious."

"Poor Shanelle, you know Shaunice will never let her live that down. They are so competitive towards one another."

Shelby's sisters were both attending a local university on athletic scholarships. They had expressed interest in physical activity since they were small children. They have participated in everything from basketball to tennis and track. Linda's home was filled with trophies and plaques celebrating their accomplishments.

"Well Mama, I'll let you go so that you can finish talking to the girls."

"Wait a minute, Shelby. You still haven't told me when you're leaving. I don't believe we finished talking about your school stuff."

"I was pretty much done. I don't know when I'm leaving yet. I haven't even decided which campus I will be attending."

Speaking it out loud made it even more real. She was actually getting out of Bethany. Her dreams were finally coming true. The more she thought about it, the more excited she became. With the way things were progressing between her and Christian, choosing Los Angeles appeared to be the obvious choice. Before she made that decision she needed to check him on that whole no contact rule of his.

Chapter Thirty-One

"That woman drives me crazy!"

Christian paced the floor and pounded his fist into his open palm. She is up to no good, whatsoever. I mean, how did she even know he would be at 1 OAK any way.

He cut his eyes at Blake. Surely his best friend wouldn't set him up like that.

"Man, you need to calm down," Blake urged.

"How did she know I would be there? I just got back in town yesterday. This doesn't make any sense. What was up with the cameras?"

Blake shook his head in disgust. "That whole situation was messed up. Man, that's the kind of stuff you see in a movie. That crap doesn't happen in real life."

"Yeah, well it did happen. Not only that, it happened to *me*."

Once again, pacing the floor, Christian pounded his fist into his hand, creating a popping sound.

Blake was growing tired of Christian's tirade. He figured Christian was making a big deal out of nothing. Sure, Alexia was wrong for pulling that stunt. Who would know, or even care. Christian was acting like he was the president or somebody important.

"Chris, you're my boy, and you know I love you."

Christian stopped pacing the floor and turned towards Blake.

"What are you trying to say, Blake?"

"Man, I think you're overreacting. You need to calm down. You're not even in the entertainment business. As a matter of fact, most people don't even know you. You'll be yesterday's news before midnight."

Christian inhaled and exhaled quickly.

"You weren't even out there. You were inside chilling, while I was being ambushed. My pupils are still burning from all of those stupid camera flashes."

Blake gave Christian a hard stare. His friend was taking things way to hard. Nothing was making sense. Obviously, Christian wasn't going to come out with his true feelings. It was up to Blake to pry it out of him. Taking a seat on the arm of the couch he turned towards his friend.

"What is this really about, Chris. You are far too upset. Help me to understand."

"Man, one of the crews that were out there had on Entertainment Media shirts. That stupid show comes on everywhere, including Bethany."

"Finally the truth. You're worried about that chick in Tennessee. I thought you said the two of you were only friends. I know you're not developing feelings for that broad."

Christian gave Blake a look similar to a child that had gotten busted by his parents.

"Man, don't call her a broad. You don't even know her. We are just friends. I don't want her to see that and get the wrong idea. She knows about me and Alexia."

Christian didn't want to give Blake too much information. Especially since he wasn't sure where he stood with Shelby. This trip home was supposed to give him some time to sort out his feeling and to know how to proceed. Unfortunately,

Alexia's stunt may have ruined any real chances he had with Shelby.

Looking at the clock on the wall, Christian noted the time. The clock displayed 1 AM which was equivalent to 3 AM in Bethany.

He stretched his arms out and yawned, in an effort to display his fatigue.

Blake was not ignorant to Christian's actions. "Man, you don't have to do all of that. I know you well enough to know when I've overstayed my welcome."

Christian laughed, "That's not it at all. I really am tired. This has been a long day. That time change is no joke either. I need to get some rest. Remember, I have that big meeting in the morning."

"Yeah okay. I'm going to head out. Give me a call sometime tomorrow or at least before you leave."

"That I can do."

Christian led Blake to the front door. Once Blake was on the other side he closed and locked the door. Walking into his bedroom he collapsed across the bed. He was sure Entertainment Media would run the story with Alexia the following day. He just hoped Shelby would not be watching.

"Alexia, if you have ruined my chances with Shelby, you will pay. I promise you that," he threatened as if she could hear him.

Chapter Thirty-Two

Shelby pressed the Power button on the television remote and set the channel. Her favorite talk show was due to come on in a little while. She picked her tablet up and returned her attention to the Fashion Institute's website. Although her campus choice appeared to be obvious, she wanted to look at each location to make an informed decision.

Studying everything from campus amenities to housing, transportation, and entertainment her anticipation grew. She couldn't believe she was finally moving forward. No longer would she have to settle for a manager's position at someone else's store. She would be gaining the skills and knowledge she needed to start her own business. Only God knew where her life was heading.

"The sky is the limit!" she yelled. Tapping her feet on the couch cushions.

Her phone rang, drawing her attention. She looked around the room before realizing she had left the phone in the kitchen. She hurried into the kitchen to catch the call before it transferred to voicemail.

"Hello," she answered almost breathless.

"Girl, what are you doing?" Dominique asked teasingly.

"Ha ha," Shelby remarked.

"I had to run and catch the phone before it went

to voicemail. Had I known it was you, I wouldn't have bothered."

"Wow, Shelby that's cold." Dominique tried to sound hurt.

"Girl, you know I'm just messing with you. What's up?"

"Nothing. Nothing at all. I'm off today so I figured I'd call and catch up with you. We haven't talked since that day you called me at work."

"Oh yeah," Shelby replied laughing.

"So did you find your Prince Charming, or at least your next Mr. Moneybags?"

"You know what, y'all need to quit trippin. I'm so tired of people referring to me like I'm some kind of hooker. It don't even be like that. And for your information, Christian and I have become quite close. He's a good guy."

"Well that's good, everybody deserves to be happy including you."

"Wow, based on that remark I don't know whether to thank you, or to go off on you."

"Trust me, it was a compliment."

Shelby stepped into the living room with the phone still pressed against her ear. Suddenly images of Christian Tyler flashed across her television screen.

"Dominique, I'll have to call you back." Shelby's voice etched terror.

"Are you alright?" Dominique asked concerned.

"Yeah, I'll call you back."

Shelby disconnected the call before Dominique could protest. She plopped down on the couch and adjusted the volume of the television.

There in plain sight was Christian and some woman wrapped up in a kiss that should've been reserved for the bedroom. Shelby's mouth flew open. She quickly covered it with her hand. She couldn't believe what she was seeing. Anger erupted inside of her like a hot volcano.

"I guess now I know why he didn't want me to call him during his so-called business trip."

She grabbed a small pillow off the couch, and threw it at the television.

"Here I was thinking you were different. You're a dog, just like all the rest."

Shelby pressed the power button on the remote control and tossed it to the floor. Involuntary tears raced down her cheeks.

❀ ❀ ❀ ❀

Christian sat quietly in his office reviewing the notes from his meeting. He was happy the meeting had gone well but he couldn't shake the feeling of discontent he was experiencing.

His phone began vibrating in his pocket. He pulled it out and acknowledged the caller. Relief swept over him when he realized it was his mother calling.

"Hey, Mom, how's it going?"

"What is the meaning of this!" Iris yelled into the phone.

Sitting up straight, Christian attempted to calm his mother.

"Wait a minute. Mom, why are you so upset."

"Why and I so upset, are you kidding me? I'm sitting here minding my own business when all of a sudden I see my son, the one I raised, all over the television wrapped up in a lip lock with that hussy Alexia."

Christian's heart sank. He felt like he could melt into the chair.

"Mom it's not what you think."

"What do you mean, it's not what I think. It's all over the television. There isn't a thing wrong with my eyes. I know what I saw."

Christian attempted to explain to his mother what really had happened. Unfortunately, his explanation fell on deaf ears. Iris wouldn't let him get a word in. She had formed an opinion based on what she saw and there was nothing he could say to make her believe otherwise. He listened to her rant for several more minutes before using his business as an excuse to end the call.

Iris was hesitant but she didn't fight him on it. Christian was ready for this nightmare to be over.

Placing his elbows on the desk, he rested his head in his hands. He could feel an instant headache developing. Suddenly it hit him. If his mother saw it, then there was a good chance that Shelby had also seen the report.

There was no telling what kind of damage this would do to their budding relationship. Disregarding his previous decision to distance himself from Shelby for a few days, he picked up his phone and dialed her number.

The phone rang, and he waited.

Chapter Thirty-Three

Staring down at the ringing phone, Shelby rolled her eyes. Why was he calling her? He had to know she didn't want anything to do with him. There was nothing he could say to her. If she never spoke to him again it would be fine with her.

The first set of rings ended and were immediately followed by a second set. *Enough of this*, she thought.

Reaching down, she pressed the ignore button on her phone and walked away from it. Hopefully he would get the hint and stop calling.

Christian listened to the familiar voicemail greeting and dropped his head. He no longer had any doubt that Shelby had seen the story about him and Alexia. He slammed his palm on his desktop sending the sound echoing throughout his office.

Shantrice pushed open his office door and gave him a blank stare.

"What is going on in here? Are you alright?" she asked.

"No, I'm not alright. I'm so sick of that woman I don't know what to do."

Shantrice stepped inside and closed the door. She walked over to the small refrigerator located in the corner of Christian's office and grabbed a bottle of water. Walking back towards his desk she held the bottle out to him.

"I'm going to need something a lot stronger than that."

"Well, this is all you have. Now tell me what's going on." She took a seat in one of the plush chairs facing his desk.

"Alexia,"

Rolling her eyes, Shantrice blew out a hard breath. "What is she up to now?"

Christian filled Shantrice in on the details of the previous night. He then shared with her the phone call he received from his mother. He felt defeated and it showed.

Shantrice hated seeing her boss and friend looking so sad. She and Christian had worked together for a long time. She initially was against his relationship with Alexia, but he convinced her Alexia was the one for him. When things fell apart she was there to help him pick up the pieces. At times they seemed more like brother and sister, than employer and employee.

Christian was there for her when she endured a horrible breakup with her ex. When she finally found the man of her dreams, he was there to walk her down the aisle. Now she believed he needed her again.

"Okay, Christian, I can understand your being upset about her basically using you. I'm sure Iris gave you an earful, but I feel like there is something you're not telling me. You are a little more upset than I would expect you to be. What is it that you're not saying?"

Feeling exposed and looking defeated, Christian opened the bottle of water and took a big gulp. He was finally going to admit his true feelings for Shelby.

"I met somebody," he said barely above a whisper.

"Say what!" Shantrice exclaimed.

"I met a woman in Bethany, and she and I have become quite close. I told her I wouldn't be contacting her, or answering my phone while I was here. Now that this has happened, she's sure to think Alexia is the reason for my no contact rule."

Shantrice looked at him like he had lost his mind. Why in the world would he make up such an absurd rule to a woman he was interested in?

"That's crazy, Christian. I mean I understand what you're saying about things between you and Alexia being innocent, but as a woman, I can guarantee she's not going to believe that. Besides, why would you come up with such a dumb rule?"

"I didn't expect all of this to happen. I tried calling her after my mom called me because I'm sure it aired around the same time there that it did here."

"What did she say?"

"She didn't say anything, she let the call go to voicemail. I feel like I'm stuck in a trap."

Shantrice folded her arms across her chest. "You know I love you, but I'll have to admit you messed up this time. Basically all we can do is hope for the best. Maybe she would rather talk to you face-to-face than over the phone. There's still hope for you."

Christian set up straight as if he had just gotten a brilliant idea. What Shantrice said made sense. Maybe there was still hope for him and Shelby. One thing was for sure he couldn't resolve it from Los Angeles, he needed to get back to Bethany.

"Change my flight, I need to get back to Bethany today."

Shantrice looked at her watch. "Okay, but you may not get there until this evening."

"It doesn't matter, the sooner the better. Make it happen."

Christian stood and walked around his desk. He continued to the office door and swung it open. Nodding his head in Shantrice's direction, he quickly clapped his hands twice.

"Chop, chop," he beckoned with a grin on his face. "Operation get the girl is in full effect."

Shantrice couldn't help but laugh at his antics. She moved to the other side of the door and shook her head.

"You are so corny, Christian."

Chapter Thirty-Four

.

"What are you doing here?"

Shelby asked blocking the door. She was not in the mood for this man or his antics. She thought he had gotten the hint to leave her alone, but apparently he had not.

"Oh, so it's like that? You're just going to leave me standing out here?"

Placing his foot in the door, he blocked Shelby from closing it.

"What do you want? Why are you here?"

"I want to talk to you. We need to clear the air."

"We don't need to clear anything, Thaddeus. If you don't leave right now I'm going to push the panic button on my alarm. The police will be here before you get off the doorstep."

Thaddeus kicked the door. He honestly didn't know why he was still pursuing Shelby. She was after all the woman that tried to single-handedly destroy his family's business. Maybe it's because he actually had to chase her, unlike most of the women he dated. Everyone in Bethany knew about his family's wealth. Finding a woman that was genuinely interested in him had not been easy. Becoming involved with Shelby would also be a good way to upset his family. His father had dictated his life since childhood. A relationship with Shelby would be the biggest blow to him.

"So you're really not going to let me in?" Thaddeus asked feigning disappointment.

"I'm not playing with you, Thaddeus. You have two seconds before I push this button."

Shelby covered the panic button with her index finger. She figured if he saw her hand on the alarm keypad he would take her threat seriously.

"Fine, you win. I'm growing tired of this little game of yours anyway. When you get ready for a real man, you know where to find me."

Thaddeus turned and headed towards his car. He could tell he was wearing her down. It was only a matter of time before he would add her to his list of conquest. There was no way he would lose out to some building contractor. Thaddeus adjusted his jacket and smiled at the thought as he opened his car door and climbed inside.

Christian gripped the steering wheel tightly as he peered at Thaddeus through squinted eyes. Anger threatened to overtake him. He wanted to wipe that smug look off Thaddeus' face. He couldn't believe it. He had cut his trip short, leaving Los Angeles without a peep. It wasn't until he was at the airport that he even let his mother know he was leaving. He drove like a madman down I- 40 hoping to get to Bethany before it was too late. Only to find Thaddeus Bierman leaving Shelby's house.

No wonder she had ignored his calls. She obviously had already moved on. Who was he kidding, Thaddeus had made his involvement with Shelby known all along. Christian felt like a fool.

All the way from the airport he looked forward to the moment he would lay eyes on Shelby. When he turned onto her street his heart began to race. He didn't know how she would react to him. He noticed the extra car in her driveway so he decided to pull across the street and turn his car off. Unsure of how she would react to the Entertainment Media story he figured he would just wait until her company left. He had no idea Thaddeus would be the person leaving her home.

Christian started his car and pulled away from the curb. He felt like he had been kicked in the stomach.

Pushing aside feelings of disappointment He decided the best thing for him to do was to pour himself into his work. He must have been crazy thinking he could actually have a relationship with a woman so far from home anyway.

Tomorrow was a new day, he would complete the task at hand and count the days until he could leave this God forsaken place. From now on he would focus all of his attention on the youth center. It was only a few more weeks before he would be returning home.

❀ ❀ ❀ ❀

Shelby watched from her bedroom window as Thaddeus got into his car and left. As much as she hated to admit it, she was becoming quite afraid of him. It's a good thing he believed her when she said she would alert the police if he didn't leave. Had he continue to pursue her, he would have realized her alarm system was not linked to an emergency service. She figured her home was in a good neighborhood and most people in Bethany knew her so there was no need to pay for an alarm system. She was already reconsidering that decision.

The lights from Thaddeus' vehicle quickly disappeared from her driveway. She noticed another car pull out after him, but it was too dark outside to identify it.

Could that be? She ended the question to herself just as quickly as she had started it. There was no way Christian could have been outside her home. He wasn't due back from Los Angeles for at least another day or two. Shelby rubbed her arms quickly with her hands attempting to ward off a cold chill. *This night is way too creepy,* she thought.

Sitting down at her dining room table she turned on her computer and continued her research on The Fashion Institute. After Christian's betrayal the last thing she wanted was to move to Los Angeles. On one hand she felt like she was being ridiculous, as large as the city was the odds were greater against her seeing him than they were for it. On the other hand, seeing him with the woman that supposedly broke his heart would be too painful.

It seemed ridiculous for her to allow his actions to dictate her decision. Right now she was extremely emotional and she knew any decision she made would be based purely on emotion. She had wanted this her entire life. She would be a fool to let the opportunity pass her by.

Grabbing a pen and paper, she wrote down pros and cons for each location. There was no need in stressing herself out. She still had time to make a final decision.

Once she had completed her list, she laid the pen down and turned the computer off.

The clock on her phone displayed 12:51am. She had no idea she had been sitting that long. Her body ached, and fatigue clouded her mind.

Shuffling her feet, Shelby walked into her bedroom.

Relieving herself of the excess clothing she climbed between the sheets. Her mind drifted to Christian.

A lone tear escaped her eye. In her heart she wanted to believe none of what she saw on the television was true.

However, her heart couldn't overrule what her eyes had seen. She stared into the darkness of the bedroom until she was overtaken by sleep.

Chapter Thirty-Five

The atmosphere around the office was tense. Christian grabbed a folder from the file cabinet and slammed the drawer. He took the folder back to his desk and threw it down. Pulling his chair out he plopped down in the chair and examined the contents of the folder.

Deborah watched Christian from across the room. His entire attitude seemed to have changed since his trip to California. He was still professional when it came to things related to the building, but he seemed so unhappy. She wanted to talk to him about it but figured she should talk to her husband first. He no longer played music in the office, and he worked extremely late hours. She figured he was no longer involved with Shelby because no one had seen them around town together lately.

"Christian, I'm going to lunch. I'll be back in a little while."

For the first time in what seemed like the entire work day Christian looked up. He looked at Deborah like he was surprised to see her standing there.

"I'm sorry, were you saying something?" He asked sincerely.

Deborah raised her left eyebrow as if she couldn't believe what she had heard. "Wow, you really are buried into your work. I was just telling you that I'm heading out to lunch. Would you like for me to bring you anything?"

"That would be great. I was planning to work through lunch anyway. Will you bring me back a burger?" Christian asked pulling out a ten-dollar bill from his wallet.

"Sure no problem." Deborah replied taking the folded currency from his hands.

❈ ❈ ❈ ❈

Deborah sat across from Daniel with a solemn expression. She was genuinely concerned about Christian. It was in her heart to help others, and he was no exception.

"What's with the long face, sweetheart?" Daniel asked.

"Actually I was just thinking about Christian."

"Come again?" Daniel trusted his wife, but he didn't know why she was spending their lunch date thinking about Christian.

Deborah looked at the sour expression on her husband's face, and burst into laughter.

"Calm down, babe. I don't mean like that. I'm kind of concerned about him. For the last two and a half weeks he's been moping around the office. He doesn't even seem like the same man. Something must have happened in California. Has he said anything to you or the other guys, when you have your dinner meetings?"

Daniel smoothed his beard with his right hand. "Now that you've mentioned it, he has been a bit reserved. Whatever it is I'm sure he'll be okay."

Deborah picked up a fry and dipped it in a small cup of ketchup.

"So he hasn't said anything during your time together?"

"Sweetheart, we're men. We don't sit around talking about our feelings."

Rolling her eyes, Deborah decided to let it go. She

clearly wasn't going to get anywhere with Daniel.

"Well, I'm going to say this and I'm done. I'm going to talk to him and find out what's going on."

"Tread lightly, baby. I wouldn't dare try to stop you because I know it won't do any good anyway. You have this internal need to play matchmaker to everyone. Christian is a private person. He's not going to want you digging too deeply into his business."

Nodding her head in agreement, Deborah turned her attention back to her meal. She was determined to find out what was going on with Christian if it was the last thing she did.

Daniel and Deborah concluded their meal over light conversation. They discussed the completion of the center, and their excitement over all the families they would help.

Deborah ordered Christian's meal and prepared to return to work. Standing at the counter she noticed Shelby enter the restaurant. Her feet seemed to have a mind of their own as she walked in Shelby's direction. She wasn't sure what she would say to her, but she genuinely wanted to know if she and Christian were still involved.

Waving her hands Deborah approached Shelby. Shelby looked at her with a perplexed expression. She couldn't figure out why Deborah was so intent on gaining her attention. They weren't what anyone would consider friends. Shelby knew Deborah worked with Christian. Curiosity got the best of her so she waved back.

"Hey Shelby, girl. How are you doing?" Deborah asked. Her tone was jovial.

"I'm well, thank you."

Deborah could tell from Shelby's reaction she was trying to figure out the purpose of their conversation. She was beginning to rethink her decision to approach her. She knew the right thing to do would be to leave her alone. Her mouth moved involuntarily. She had to find a way to have a small conversation without making Shelby feel uncomfortable.

"I'm glad I saw you today. As I'm sure you've noticed we're getting pretty close to completing the youth center. Daniel and I were thinking it would be a good idea to have a cookout in celebration. You were very generous with your donation to our efforts and I think it would be great if you attended."

Shelby was confused. Based on the size of the youth center she was sure it cost more than a million dollars to build. She didn't know in what world her twenty-five-dollar donation was considered generous.

"Congratulations on your building. I'm not sure I'll be able to attend the cookout. I do wish you all the best."

"But I haven't given you the date yet." Deborah protested.

"I realized that, but I have a lot going on right now." Shelby stated matter-of-factly.

Taking the hint to back off, Deborah smiled gently.

"I understand. The invitation is open in case something changes. If it's okay with you I'll mail the details to your house."

"That'll be fine." Shelby took a step back. "I don't mean to be rude, but I have an appointment to keep."

"Of course. I didn't mean to keep you."

Deborah allowed Shelby to pass. The cashier waved at her to get her attention. She retrieved Christian's meal and left the restaurant. Hurriedly, she joined Daniel in the car.

"What took you so long?" Daniel asked as he backed

out of the parking spot.

"I was waiting on Christian's order." She answered feigning innocence.

"I saw you talking to Shelby. I hope you're not trying to play matchmaker."

"Of course not, dear. By the way we need to plan a cookout."

Daniel looked at his wife and shook his head. He knew when she got an idea in her head there was no stopping her. He was certain that she was cooking up a major scheme. He just hoped it wouldn't backfire in her face.

Deborah smiled broadly at Daniel and patted him on his knee. Her conversation with Shelby had given her all the information she needed.

Returning to the office she handed Christian his lunch. He looked like he had not moved an inch since she left the office. She needed to get him out of that foul mood he was in.

"Here's your lunch," she said handing him the bag.

"Thanks," he replied without looking up.

Deborah decided to press him a bit. She wasn't sure how he would react. Hopefully she would improve his mood and put the smile on his face that had been missing.

"I saw Shelby at the restaurant," she said.

Christians head shot straight up, he stared at her with fiery eyes. She had gotten his message loud and clear before he ever uttered a word.

"That's no surprise, this is a small town everyone is bound to run into each other at some point."

Deborah struggled to ignore his tone. Forcing out a strained giggle she replied, "I'm sure that's true. I was surprised because I know she works in Jackson. Then again, I don't know her work schedule. I just thought you'd like to know that I saw her. I know the two of you have been seeing each other."

"Then perhaps you should be having this conversation with Thaddeus," Christian snapped.

Christian was immediately remorseful. Deborah was only trying to have a conversation with him and he was being a complete jerk. Not only that she and Daniel had only shown him kindness for as long as he had been in Bethany. She didn't deserve the way he was treating her.

"I'm sorry Deborah. I was way out of line."

"It's okay, I understand. I am confused about something though."

"What's that?"

"You mentioned Thaddeus. I don't know very many men by that name, especially here in Bethany. Surely you can't be referring to Thaddeus Bierman."

Christian looked at her oddly. "That's exactly who I'm referring to. Why does that surprise you."

Deborah grabbed the chair from her desk, and placed it next to Christians. She could see that it was time to fill Mr. Hollywood in on the town's secrets.

Chapter Thirty-Six

Shelby pulled in front of her mother's home and parked her car. She was looking forward to their monthly lunch date. Normally Linda would prepare a meal for them, but Shelby had insisted on bringing their lunch. Her mother loved the burgers at Hattie's Place restaurant, but she only ate there on rare occasions. Shelby knew this would be an awesome surprise.

Linda pulled open the front door before Shelby could raise her hand to knock. She greeted her eldest daughter with a huge smile and warm embrace. The aroma from their meals seeped through the tiny space between them. Linda inhale deeply. Stepping back from her daughter she looked at the bag in her hand.

"Is that what I think it is?" she asked with a sheepish grin.

"Yes it is, and I got it just the way you like it with grilled onions, two slices of cheese, lettuce, pickles and extra tomato."

"Honey chile, I'm about to put a hurting on this." Linda exclaimed grabbing the bag out of her daughter's hand.

Shelby laughed aloud as she watched her mother bounce into the kitchen. She was grateful for the time she was able to spend with her mother alone. As much as she was looking forward to starting school, it was moments like these that she would miss the most. No matter what kind of day she was having, she could count on her mother to do something humorous to cheer her up.

Linda placed two plates on the table, and distributed the contents of the bag. Next, she grabbed two glasses from the cabinet and filled them with ice. She reached into the refrigerator and pulled out a container of sweetened iced tea and lemonade. She filled each glass halfway with tea, and finish them off with lemonade.

Shelby shook her glass slightly to further mix the beverage. She turned her glass up and took a big swallow.

"Ooh mama this is so good. This is my all-time favorite drink."

Linda grabbed her daughter's hand and offered a quick prayer of thanks. She then picked up a sandwich and took a huge bite.

"Slow down, Mama. I have my own sandwich. I'm not going to take yours. Make sure you come up for air."

Linda swatted at her like she was a fly and continued enjoying her meal. She noticed Shelby was taking longer to eat her food than normal. She knew her daughter well enough to know something was bothering her. Wiping her face and hands on a napkin, she took a swallow from her glass to wash her food down.

"What's wrong, baby?"

Shelby and her mother maintained a very open relationship. Shelby never tried to hide anything she was dealing with from her mom. Throughout her adult life she had come to find that her mother gave the best advice with issues she was dealing with especially matters of the heart.

"My day started out fine actually. Then, I ran into Deborah Joseph at the restaurant and now my mind is all over the place."

Linda looked at Shelby perplexed. "Why would seeing Deborah, throw your day off. I didn't think the two of you were friends nor enemies."

"We're not," Shelby answered honestly. "She works with Christian."

"Oh, I see." Linda replied giving Shelby a sidelong glance. "So I take it you still have not talked to him."

"No I haven't. Truthfully, I wouldn't even know what to say."

"Like I've always told you Shelby, don't overthink everything. Sometimes even the things you see with your own eyes can be deceiving. You will never find your true answers until you talk to the person directly. From there you take what you've seen, and what the person says and weigh them out. Your heart will give you the right answer."

"You're probably right." Shelby answered solemnly.

"Of course I'm right." Linda stood and cleared the dishes from the table. "Now that that's out of the way, what did Deborah want with you anyway?"

"She wanted to invite me to a cookout they are having in honor of the youth center being completed. I guess they're pretty close to finishing."

"Now that you've mentioned it, I believe I read something in the paper saying they'll be finished in a couple weeks."

"Yeah well, I told her I was busy."

"I think you should go. That may be the perfect opportunity for you to talk to Christian in a neutral territory."

"I don't know, Mom. I'm not sure I'm ready to talk to him. Then again, he may not want to talk to me. I haven't heard from him at all since he returned from California, and that's been a few weeks."

Linda furrowed her eyebrows. Something about this entire situation was strange. Although she didn't know the extent of Shelby's relationship with Christian, within her heart she felt like he and Shelby needed to talk. No matter the outcome she would always support her daughter. In her opinion, this situation needed some Divine intervention.

Chapter Thirty-Seven

Shelby pulled the invitation from Deborah out of her mailbox and studied it intently. Her mother had convinced her to attend the cookout. She only had a few days to prepare, but she was determined to have an outfit that would make Christian stop in his tracks. He needed to know what he would be missing out on.

Returning to the house, Shelby tossed the mail on the kitchen counter and washed her hands. She was expecting Kim at any moment. She decided to fix Philly steak sandwiches for them while she waited for her friend to arrive.

Shelby reached into the refrigerator and gathered the necessary ingredients. With all of the ingredients in place she put a few drops of olive oil into a hot skillet. She carefully added the shredded steak, onion, and bell pepper. Once the meat was done, she added cheese and filled the two awaiting rolls. The doorbell rang just as she was placing the sandwiches on the plates.

She hurried to the door and opened it. Kim was all smiles as she hugged her best friend and kissed her cheek. Shelby returned the sentiment. Entering into the kitchen Kim took a deep breath.

"It smells so good in here," she stated smiling broadly. "What are you cooking?" she asked.

"I thought I'd fix us some Phillies. In fact, you're just in time to choose between French fries and potato chips."

Shelby held up a bag of frozen French fries and cheese potato chips. Kim looked around the kitchen and noticed the sandwiches were plated. She grabbed the potato chips out of Shelby's hand and pulled the bag open.

"I think we should have these since the sandwiches are already done." Kim said as she darted off to the bathroom to wash her hands. She returned and placed several chips on each of the plates.

Shelby pulled a jug of lemonade out of the refrigerator. She grabbed two glasses from the cabinet and added ice to each one.

"That works for me. Let's take this stuff into the dining room."

Each lady grabbed a plate of food and a glass of lemonade and headed to the table. Shelby was delighted to see her friend. She didn't know what was going on with Kim, but she noticed her friend's attitude was more upbeat than the last time she saw her. Shelby was excited to get the conversation going. They had a lot of ground to cover before Kim would have to leave to meet her children's school bus. Grabbing a napkin, she wiped her mouth and took a small sip of lemonade.

"So girl, tell me what's going on with you. You're looking really good." Shelby complemented.

Kim started blushing. She held up her index finger signaling to Shelby to give her a moment while she finished her bite. Once she was done she displayed a full blown grin.

"Things are going pretty good. And let me tell you, it's all because of the Lord. Because me, I would have done things totally different had I not prayed about it. My husband has been trying very hard to make things up to me. We even started going to marriage counseling. We also have instituted a date night. My mother-in-law has agreed to look after the children for us at least twice a month so that he and I can have some alone time."

Shelby admired her friend. She knew the decision Kim had made was a struggle for her. There were many women that probably would have ended their marriage immediately, but Kim was a fighter. Before the cheating occurred, they seemed to have a good relationship. Shelby didn't know if she would be able to have that kind of strength if she were in Kim's position.

"I'm glad to hear that things are better. You are a sweetheart Kim, and you deserve to be happy."

"Thank you, Shell. Now that's enough about me. What's going on with you? I feel like we haven't talked in a while."

Shelby filled her in on the latest gossip, and her acceptance into The Fashion Institute. She told her she was struggling to make a decision on the location she should choose. The time was winding down and she didn't have much more time to procrastinate. Shelby finished up her meal and dusted the crumbs from her hands.

"What about Christian? Have you talked to him yet?"

Shelby cast her eyes down towards the table. Her shoulders slumped slightly at the mention of his name. She was missing him more than she realized. In a way she was glad Deborah had invited her to the cookout. If nothing else she would have an opportunity to feast her eyes on the handsome man from California.

"Unfortunately no. I haven't seen or spoken with him since he returned from Los Angeles. I'm going to a cookout this weekend sponsored by the Josephs'. it's in celebration of the completion of the center, so I'm pretty sure he'll be there."

Kim noticed the change in her friend's demeanor. They had been friends long enough for Kim to know when Shelby was serious about something or someone. Therefore, she knew her friend had developed strong feelings for Christian.

Reaching her hand across the table, she patted Shelby on the back of the hand. "Hold your head up, girlfriend. Everything is going to work out exactly as it should. Watch and see."

Shelby met Kim's gaze. With all of her heart, she wanted that to be true.

Pushing her chair back from the table Kim stood and extended her hand to Shelby. "Now, show me what you're planning to wear."

Taking Kim's hand, she rose from her seat. "Why certainly, madam. Right this way." Shelby answered in a British accent.

Chapter Thirty-Eight

The cookout was in full swing. Waves of hickory smoke moved throughout the pavilion. Bouquets of balloons served as centerpieces on each table. Children played freely engaging one another in games of tag and red light green light. The food was on display buffet style. The line of food included hot dogs, burgers, chicken, ribs, baked beans, macaroni and cheese, spaghetti, potato salad, and pasta salad. A separate table held various desserts including cakes and pies. Large coolers were filled with ice and beverages.

Daniel flipped burgers on the grill before returning to the table where Christian and Landon were engrossed in a game of Dominoes.

Deborah looked at her watch and out at the parking lot. Although Shelby told her she wouldn't be able to attend the event she held out hope that she would reconsider. A few guests approached her at the food table, gaining her attention. She assisted them with their food selections before turning her attention back to the parking lot.

A smile creased her lips when she saw Shelby pull into an empty parking spot and park her car.

Deborah immediately left the table and walked over to greet her. She wrapped her arms around Shelby in a quick hug.

"I am so happy you decided to attend today." she

confessed.

"Thanks for inviting me. It looks like you all have quite a celebration going on here. And girl, I can smell the food from here." Shelby replied with a smile.

"Well, I don't mean to brag, but you know Daniel is the best grill master in Bethany."

"So I've heard," Shelby replied.

"Now you can see for yourself. Come on over here and get something to eat."

Deborah grabbed Shelby by her arm and led her towards the pavilion. Christian stood to his feet as Landon claimed another victory.

"Here Daniel, you can have my spot. That's enough butt whippings for me. I think Landon is just trying to embarrass me now." Christian stated.

"Aww, man. Is not like that. I tried to tell you I got skills." Landon teased.

"Yeah, okay. You all go ahead and play, I'm going to use my skills on these ribs."

Christian turned towards the food table and noticed Shelby approaching. He stood motionless as she got closer to him. She wore a spaghetti strapped peach colored jumpsuit. He would have sworn she had designed it herself because it fit her perfectly. Nude colored strappy sandals showed off her pedicured feet.

"Hello Christian," Shelby greeted when she got closer to him.

"Shelby, hi." He responded.

An undeniable passion radiated from them. Anyone watching them would know they had a special connection. Christian felt as if he had been given a prize. Finding his voice, he spoke up.

"This is quite a surprise. I wasn't expecting to see you here today."

"Yeah, I can tell by your expression," she replied. "Deborah invited me."

"Oh, I see. In that case, I'm glad you accepted her invitation."

"I keep hearing about Daniel Joseph's barbecue. I figured this was as good a time as any to finally try it."

"Is that so?" Christian said nodding his head. "I guess there's no better time than the present. I was heading over to the table myself. If you don't mind, I'd love to share a meal with you and talk to you."

"Sure, why not," she answered softly.

Christian and Shelby filled their plates.

He reached into the cooler and retrieved beverages for both of them. He gave Deborah a quick wink as an appreciative gesture. Normally he didn't like for people to interfere in his personal life, but in this case it was just what he needed. He pointed to a table in the corner away from everyone.

"Would you mind sitting over there?" he asked Shelby.

"It looks like the perfect spot to me," she replied grateful for the small piece of privacy.

They sat down in initial silence.

Neither wanted to be the first to speak. A small level of tension settled between them.

Shelby picked up a small rib and took a bite.

"Mmmm, this *is* delicious," she moaned in delight.

"I told you it was good," Christian said before taking a bite of chicken.

"It really is as good as everyone says. I wonder what his secret is."

"Trust me, that secret is as secure as the U.S. Mint. I'm sure it is hidden in a steel vault."

"You're probably right." Shelby laughed and licked the sauce off her fingertips.

Christian was glad to see that she appeared to be having a good time. Now that she was more relaxed, he felt it would be a good time for them to talk. There was no sense in procrastinating any further.

"So, Shelby, how have you been?" he asked.

"I've been okay." She answered in an upbeat tone. She didn't want to give him any indication of how much she had missed him.

"Oh, okay." He said, sounding surprised.

"What about you? How have you been?" Shelby asked before taking another bite of food.

"I guess you could say I've been okay. I've been working hard, and pretty much trying to figure things out."

"I can understand that. I've had a lot to think about myself."

Shelby wanted to remain cordial, but she was upset. She could not believe that he didn't have the decency to call or come by to see her after he returned from California. Even if what she saw about him and Alexia were true, the least he could have done was call her and explain. To show her displeasure, she figured she would speak directly concerning the situation.

"How was your trip back home?" she asked in a sharp and uneasy tone.

Christian noticed the tone, but he did not want to speculate on the reason behind it. His mind immediately went to the Entertainment Media report. He figured she was upset about what she had seen. He decided the best way to turn the conversation in his favor was to bring up the report first.

"Actually the trip was very upsetting for me. My friend Blake wanted to go and hangout as a way of welcoming me home, but my ex showed up out of nowhere. She even had the nerve to kiss me in front of reporters trying to make it appear as though we were a couple. I was so upset that I didn't even stay at the club. I had Blake to take me home. The next day, shortly after my meeting I had my assistant to change my flight and I came back to Bethany."

Shelby looked Christian in his eyes. She was trying to discern whether or not he was telling the truth. She still couldn't understand why he chose to not contact her. Things between them before he left had been great. None of it made sense.

"Wow, I guess that's some real Hollywood drama."

"Yeah, drama I don't care to be a part of. What the cameras didn't catch was my reaction to her."

"That's crazy." Shelby placed her fork down on her plate and looked directly into Christian eyes. She needed answers. She knew being passive was not the way to get the answers that she desired.

"Christian, I can understand you being upset about her actions anyone would be. Especially if you don't have any feelings for her. What I don't understand is why you chose to cut me off? I thought things were going pretty good between us before you left, but once you got back I didn't hear from you anymore. That's not how you treat someone you care about. Unless of course you really don't care about me in that way."

He dropped his head. Shelby was right. Even though he was upset over seeing Thaddeus leave her home, as a

man he should have called her on it. He didn't want to be
judged on the actions of Alexia, but he had done the exact
same thing to Shelby. His heart went out to her.

Christian reached for her hand but she pulled back.

"Shelby, sweetheart I owe you an apology. There
is however something you should know. While I was in
L.A., you were all I could think about. When Alexia pulled
that stunt my main concern was I hoped you didn't see it
because I didn't want you to think there was anything going
on between she and I. I tried calling you, but the calls went
to your voicemail. That's when I decided to return early.
When I arrived back in Bethany I came straight to your
house. I wanted to explain what had happened with Alexia
in person."

Shelby's eyes widened, Christian could tell he had her
full attention. Her silence gave him the nudge to go on.

"When I pulled up at your home, I saw Thaddeus
leaving. He had a wide grin on his face and he was
adjusting his jacket. I thought that the two of you had been
together. I mean he had been dropping hints to me about
you since I got here. It was just too much to deal with so
I withdrew. I poured myself into my work, and I've been
counting the days until I return home for good."

Shelby rolled her eyes and folded her arms in protest.
"There is not now, nor has there ever been anything going
on between me and Thaddeus Bierman. That man has
been a problem for me for as long as I can remember."

Christian reached for her once again. Shelby
surrendered and allowed him to hold her hand.

"I didn't know it at the time, but I know that now. A
short while ago Deborah and I were at work talking and
she decided to fill me in on some of the town's history.

Particularly the history of Thaddeus and his sense of entitlement."

"Is that so?" Shelby asked, softening towards him.

"Yes, sweetheart it is so. I'm sorry you've had to go through that."

Christian stared at her passionately. He wanted so badly to pull her into his arms, to protect her, and to show her how much he truly cared for her. Releasing her hand, he gathered their plates and tossed them into the nearby trash. Returning to the table he pulled Shelby up from her seat.

"Would you mind if we got out of here? I mean maybe we could go somewhere and talk in private, without people constantly looking at us trying to figure out what we're talking about."

"I think that's a great idea. I'm going to thank Deborah for inviting me and then we can go."

"That'll work. While you talk to Deborah, I'll let Daniel know I'm leaving as well. We still have plenty of daylight left. I would love to go back to that lake where you and I picnicked."

Chapter Thirty-Nine

Shelby looked at Christian and smiled. She inserted the key into her front door and turned it. The two stepped inside.

"Thank you for agreeing to come over to my house instead of the lake. When I told Deborah I was leaving, she loaded me up with food. I didn't want to leave it in the car."

"It's not a problem. She did the same thing to me," he stated lifting the containers in his hands.

Christian took the two containers of food and placed them on the kitchen counter. He remained stationary until Shelby led him into the living room. The past few weeks away from her had been quite lonely. Although he had hoped they would somehow work things out, he was doubtful. Now, being in her home he felt a glimmer of hope.

"You can have a seat on the couch, unless you prefer the chair." Shelby offered nervously.

"This will be fine," Christian answered while taking a seat on the couch.

"Would you like something to drink?" she offered.

"No," Christian reached up and pulled Shelby down next to him. "I don't want anything but you sitting next to me."

Shelby smiled and complied to his wishes. She didn't know why she was so uptight. As much as she wanted him there with her, she still wondered if what he told her about Alexia was the complete truth.

Sensing her resolve, he grabbed her hand and gently massaged her palm. He felt her relaxing at his touch.

Christian was determined to show Shelby how much she meant to him. The time he spent away from her showed him how much he truly cared for her. Shelby let out a soft moan.

"Sweetheart, tell me what I've missed while we were apart."

She turned towards him and shrieked. "You go first. My news is major, and I'd hate to overshadow you." She teased.

Christian grabbed his chin and rubbed it vigorously. He smirked. "Since you put it like that, I'll make this quick. I already told you about my trip to L.A. Once I returned to Bethany, I threw myself into work and I hit the gym quite a bit."

Shelby squeezed his bicep. "I guess I feel a little something going on here."

"Get off me, woman," Christian said, pulling his arm out of her reach.

The two burst into laughter. They laughed as if they had never spent a moment apart. This was what they needed. Their time together was always enjoyable. It was as if they were meant to be together.

Turning serious, Christian pulled Shelby's face towards him and kissed her passionately.

She wrapped her arms around him and shared the moment. He smoothed her hair and continued to envelop her lips with his. He felt like he could kiss her lips forever.

Shelby broke their embrace. She leaned back against

the couch, slightly pulling away from him.

"I'm sorry, I didn't mean to make you uncomfortable."

A smile creased her lips. "It's not that at all. Trust me, that has been the highlight of my day. However, if we keep doing that I will never get to tell you my news.

"I guess you have a point." Christian sat back and turned towards her. "I'm all ears, tell me what's going on with you."

Shelby jumped up from the couch and went to her bedroom.

She returned waving an envelope and bouncing up and down. She extended the envelope to Christian.

"Read it."

"Okay." Christian looked at her with an odd expression. He pulled the letter from the envelope and started to read it.

"I got in, I got in." Shelby yelled while clapping her hands.

Christian stood up beside her and hugged her. "That's awesome, sweetheart. I'm so happy for you." Turning serious he sat back on the couch. "The letter said you would have to choose the campus location you will attend. Have you made a decision?"

Shelby plopped down on the couch. "Not yet. I have another week to decide. Classes will start in about a month."

"Are you leaning more towards any particular location? I noticed they have a campus in Los Angeles."

"I'm weighing my options. Nothing's set in stone yet."

"I see. Of course you know which city get's my vote."

Shelby placed her finger over her lips. "Hmm, New York?"

"Very funny. You know I want you to be in Los Angeles with me."

She fell silent. Words escaped her. Could what he was saying to her be true or was he just saying what he thought she wanted to hear? Things were growing intense and she wasn't sure she was ready for this. Could she really ignore the time they had spent apart? If Alexia made a move on him once, who's to say she wouldn't do it again.

"Christian, I don't know. I have a lot to think about. This is moving a little fast for me."

"Wait a minute, Shelby. I don't want to overwhelm you or make you feel rushed. This has been a full day. Perhaps I should go. We can get together again soon." Christian stood to leave.

"You don't have to go. Besides, we still have leftovers to enjoy."

"I'll take my plate to go." He grabbed her by her hands and pulled her up next to him. He kissed her on each cheek. "Don't worry sweetheart I won't let anything come between us like I did before."

Shelby wanted to protest but decided against it. He was right, the day had been quite full and she didn't want to make decisions based on emotion. She followed him to the front door so that he could leave. She handed him his food container off the counter.

He turned and gave her a kiss. "I'll call you when I make it home if that's okay."

"I'd be offended if you didn't." She replied and closed the door behind him.

Shelby ran into her bedroom and dived into her bed.

Laying on her back she kicked her legs in the air and pounded her fist into the mattress. Her heart was pounding with excitement. The day had turned out much better than she expected. She had hoped for a conversation and some answers, but instead she got reconciliation and it felt so good. She didn't realize how much she had truly missed Christian until she was back in his arms.

Sitting up on the bed, Shelby reached for her cell phone. There was only one person she wanted to talk to, and that was her mother.

She dialed the number and waited for an answer.

Linda answer the phone cheerfully, "Hey baby, how's it going?"

"Mama, you will not believe the day I've had. I'm so glad I listened to you and went to the cookout."

"I take it you saw your fella."

"Yes I did. In fact, he just left a short while ago."

Shelby could hear her mother breathing into the phone. She knew her well enough to know that was the sound of displeasure.

"Before you start thinking crazy, nothing happened. I am not trying to put myself in that position."

"Don't act like you know your mama so well," Linda joked. "So tell me what happened."

Shelby filled her mother in on her conversations with Christian. She replayed Christian's explanation of his run-in with Alexia. She also told her about him seeing Thaddeus leave her home and assuming they had been involved.

"So are you satisfied with his explanations?" Linda asked.

"You know Mom, I am. I believe he was telling me the truth. There's no way he would have known about Thaddeus coming over had he not seen him. And as far as Alexia is concerned the timeline adds up, he would have had to come back to Bethany early in order to see Thaddeus."

"As long as you are happy, then I'm happy for you."

Shelby struggled with her words. She was trying to find a way to tell her mother her decision concerning school. She had already been leaning towards Los Angeles, and after talking to Christian she became confident with her choice.

"Mom, there is something else I need to tell you."

Linda noticed the change in Shelby's tone. She knew her daughter well enough to know that she was about to reveal a major revelation. Shelby always held things in until she was forced to reveal what was going on with her. This was one of those moments.

"Go ahead and tell me what it is. Whatever it is I'm sure I can handle it. I may not even be as surprised as you think I will."

Shelby hesitated. After a brief pause she blurted out, "I've made my decision, I'm moving to Los Angeles. I'll attend school there. I'm making this decision on my own free will without any outside influence. I know this will be the best thing for me.

"That's no surprise to me, I figured you were going to do that. When you first applied to that school you told me if you got in you would want to go to California. That was before you ever met Christian. In fact, I believe the only reason you were wrestling with your decision is because you were focusing on him. You were wondering how things would be if you chose to go to school there with the two of you not being together."

"Mama, how do you do that?" she asked sincerely.

Shelby did not understand how her mother could seemingly read her mind at times.

"Chile, I gave birth to you, it wasn't the other way around."

"You have a point there," Shelby agreed.

Linda took control of the conversation, reminding Shelby of her status as the mother. She was going to miss her baby immensely, but she didn't want to be a hindrance to her. Shelby had always set aside her desires for the sake of her family. It was her turn to pursue her dreams.

"When am I going to meet this man that has captured my baby's heart?"

"I don't know. He's supposed to call me when he makes it home. I'll mention it to him and then I'll call and let you know."

"Just make sure you make it quick, and when I say quick I mean real quick."

"Yes ma'am. Point taken and duly noted."

Shelby's phone clicked indicating a waiting call. After checking the phone, she directed her attention back to her mother. "That's him calling now. I'll give you a call back in the morning."

"Alright baby go ahead and take your call, I love you."

"I love you too, Mama. We'll talk soon."

Shelby ended the call with her mother and pressed the button to swap calls before Christian hung up.

"Hey, I take it you arrived home safely."

"Yes, as a matter of fact I did. I guess I drove a little slower than usual. I was so busy reflecting on our day together, that I didn't realize how slow I was actually driving. If felt good being with you again."

Shelby blushed. She could not continue to allow

Christian to think his feelings were one-sided. She was just as happy to be with him as he was her. They had a serious connection and she couldn't deny it.

"Okay you got me I'll admit it; I was just as happy being with you today as you were. I guess we really did miss each other."

"You didn't have to admit it, I could see it in your eyes, and I definitely felt it in your kiss. I was wondering how long we would play this game of cat and mouse."

Shelby laughed. "You could not tell."

"Oh yes I could. When we kissed, it was like we had never been apart," Christian confessed.

"You detected all of that in our kiss?"

"Sweetheart, don't you get it. It wasn't about the kiss. Our hearts are intertwined."

"Okay, if you say so." She wouldn't admit it but she knew exactly what he was talking about. She felt the same way.

"Christian, before I forget, my mom wants to meet you. She wants to know when we can make that happen."

"Oh you've been talking about me to your mom, I see."

"Yep, she wants to know who this man is that has her daughter all confused." Shelby laughed into the phone, igniting laughter from him.

"The youth center is pretty much complete. We're at the stage of going through final inspections. I'll be here until the ribbon cutting and then I'm heading back home. With that being said, I think we should set it up as soon as possible. She and I need to meet."

Shelby paused. Hearing Christian say he would be leaving in a couple of weeks caused her to really examine her feelings for him. If what they had was real, then they would be able to withstand the time apart until she starts school.

"My mom likes for us all to get together for Sunday dinner once a month. Tomorrow happens to be our date. Would you like to accompany me?"

"Of course, let me know what time you want me to pick you up. We can ride over together."

An immediate smile creased Shelby's lips. "Okay. I'll call you in the morning."

"I'll look forward to your call." He replied.

Christian and Shelby made plans to meet up the following day and ended their call. Christian could finally relax. He had his woman back.

Chapter Forty

Christian sat in the recliner in his bedroom. He and Shelby had been virtually inseparable for the past two weeks. He laughed at the recollection of her family dinner. Her mother was very kind and he knew having her as a mother-in-law would be a blessing. Shelby's sisters were not as easy. They drilled him every chance they got. When they weren't drilling him they were teasing her. Thanks to her sister Sheena he discovered he had been the first man that she had invited to their family dinner.

Christian was in love with Shelby and he felt it was time that he let her know just how much. Those that were close to him would think he was crazy but he couldn't imagine being without her. Growing up and even in his adult years he never had a real example of a loving relationship. He believed in his heart that he could change that.

Shelby was nothing like Alexia. She did not make demands on him, nor did she ask him a lot of questions concerning his business or living situation in California. Although she had never said it, she didn't seem to want anything from him but love. He could tell from their conversations that she simply wanted to be happy, and to follow her dreams with a good man by her side. It was time for him to stop holding back, and to let her know how he truly felt. He knew his friends and family would not approve of his plans, but it was his life. It was time for him to be happy.

Christian showered and put on a black two button suit, with a light gray mock neck shirt. He had asked Shelby to accompany him to the ribbon cutting ceremony.

His labor of love for the families in Bethany, Tennessee was now complete. Shantrice had already booked his flight back to Los Angeles, following his specific instructions.

Satisfied with his appearance, Christian grabbed his keys, and phone, and headed towards his car.

He sent Shelby a text message letting her know he was on his way before backing out of the parking spot. He chose not to call because he didn't want to take away from the time she was using to get ready.

Arriving at her home, he stepped out of the vehicle and walked to her front door. Christian rang the doorbell and waited for her to answer.

Shelby opened the door and caused his mouth to drop. She was dressed in a beautiful fuchsia colored skirt and jacket with a silk ivory tank top underneath. A short single stand of pearls hung from her neck. Her ears were decorated with gold earrings with a dangling pearl. Finally, she wore a single strand pearl bracelet on her left wrist. Her hair was pulled into a sleek bun with curls cascading down the left side. Her makeup consisted of nude shades that further highlighted her beauty.

"You never cease to amaze me. You are absolutely beautiful." He complimented.

Shelby couldn't help but smile. "I'm so glad you approve. Given the occasion, I figured this was my best option."

"Well you did a wonderful job," Christian replied.

Glancing down at his watch he realized they needed to

get going. He extended his arm to her, and escorted her to the car.

Once she was seated he closed her door and stepped around to the driver side. He slid inside and leaned over and kissed her on the cheek.

"Thank you for accompanying me. I really appreciate it."

"I wouldn't have it any other way," she replied.

Christian grabbed Shelby's hand, and held onto it throughout the ride. He didn't speak much. His mind was running in several different directions. He had decided to share his true feelings with Shelby following the ribbon cutting ceremony.

He also expected to see Thaddeus for the first time since learning of his treatment of Shelby. Christian's natural instinct was to protect her. If Thaddeus approached her in any way that was less than honorable, Christian wasn't sure what he would do. He whispered a silent prayer that everything would go smoothly.

Pulling onto the youth center parking lot, he noticed Daniel and Deborah along with their children standing in front of the building. Members of the Board of Directors were starting to arrive. A man who Shelby identified as the mayor of Bethany stood talking to a local news reporter.

Deborah ran over to them, and greeted them both with a hug.

"Shelby you look amazing," Deborah complimented examining her from head to toe.

"Thank you. You're pretty stunning yourself." Shelby replied referring to the gold sheath dress Deborah was wearing.

Deborah suddenly turned her nose up and rolled her

eyes. "Ump, if it ain't the devil himself."

Shelby and Christian turned to see who she was referring to. Neither was surprised when they saw Thaddeus Bierman approaching.

Dangling from his arm was a twenty something year old woman with red hair. Her short white dress looked more suitable for a music video, than for a ribbon cutting ceremony.

His wide grin revealed his satisfaction with his guest and the reaction he was getting from everyone in attendance. He walked past Shelby and Christian and nodded his head.

They chose to not respond.

Following the ribbon cutting ceremony, Christian and Shelby went back to her house.

She left him alone in the living room while she changed clothes. Keeping on the tank top, she exchanged her suit for a pair of jeans. She returned to the living room where Christian was sitting on the couch.

"What's wrong with you?" she asked while trying to read his expression.

"There's absolutely nothing wrong, sweetheart. In fact, from the moment I met you every thing has been right with me. You are an amazing woman, Shelby Lamar."

"Stop, Christian. You're going to make me blush."

"You know my time here is done. Now that the center is finished I have to return back to my real life."

Shelby turned to face him directly. Her heart started to pound. She didn't know what to expect next. Was he going to tell her that all of this had been some kind of game. Was she just someone to help him get through his time away from his life in Los Angeles? She nodded her head, but remained silent.

"From the moment I met you, Shelby my life changed. It seemed in every way possible the odds were stacked against us. It didn't make sense for a man from Los Angeles, literally the other side of the country, to fall in love with a woman from Bethany. A place that most people have never heard of."

Shelby look confused. "What did you just say, Christian?"

"You heard me correctly, I'm in love with you, Shelby, and I can't imagine my life without you. Please tell me you feel the same way."

Nodding her head, a single tear escaped her eye. "I do, Christian, I'm in love with you, too."

Christian wanted to take her in his arms, but there was something more for him to do. He reached into his inner jacket pocket and pulled out a plane ticket. "I can't imagine leaving here without you by my side. I don't ever want to lose you, again. Come home with me, Shelby."

Shelby took the ticket out of Christian's hand and studied it.

In her hand was a first class ticket to Los Angeles for *Shelby Tyler*. She blinked twice thinking she had read the ticket incorrectly.

She looked up at Christian for an explanation. Between his index finger and his thumb, he held a platinum, 3-carat, princess cut, diamond engagement ring.

He slid down to the floor and landed on his knee. He looked into her eyes and spoke sincerely.

"Shelby, I love you. From the moment I met you, I felt connected to you. I tried to fight my feelings by finding every way possible that a relationship between us wouldn't work.

The harder I fought against it, the clearer things became. I have never felt the way I feel about you. Not only do I love you, but I believe you love me as well. If you will be my wife, I promise I will pour my love into you for the rest of our lives. I will support you in your dreams, and I will be the husband, future father, and friend that you desire and deserve. Will you marry me?"

Her single tear was joined by countless others. Shelby couldn't believe this was happening to her. With all of the hurt she had experienced in her past she never thought she would find a man that would truly love her.

She leaned over and kissed him passionately.

"I love you, Christian. With everything within me, I love you. I will be honored to be your wife. Yes, I will marry you. I want to spend the rest of my life with you."

"As I do you," Christian replied placing the ring on her finger.

Shelby immediately went into bride mode and panicked. "How can we do this? How can we plan a wedding from so far away? I don't want a long engagement, but I'm starting school soon."

Christian joined Shelby on the couch. He looked her directly in her eyes. "Baby, do you truly believe I'm the man for you?"

"Of course I do."

"Then let's elope. Just you, I, God, and the Judge."

"This is crazy, Christian. Is this really happening. This seems like a dream."

"This is definitely happening. Now say yes, let's elope. We can take the money we would spend on a wedding and go on a honeymoon any where in the world you want to go."

Shelby shook her head. She couldn't believe she was even considering Christian's suggestion. "I can't believe I'm saying this, but okay, I'll do it, but on one condition, I want my mother to be there. I'm her firstborn, there's no way I would deny her the opportunity to see me get married."

"That's fine with me, give her a call."

Shelby pulled out her cell phone and dialed her mother's number. As soon as she heard her mother's greeting, she started yelling. "Mama, I'm getting married!"

Linda, responded by yelling back. "*What!*"

"Yes, Mama. Christian proposed. I am so happy. I know this is the best thing for me. Please tell me you're happy, Mama."

"Oh my God, baby. I'm so happy for you." Linda wanted her daughter to be happy more than anything in the world. Seeing them together confirmed their love for each other. She was not going to stand in their way.

Shelby recounted for her the details of Christian's proposal, and their desire to elope.

"What do you mean you're going to elope?"

"Christian thought it would be a good idea and I agreed. We don't want to wait the time it would take to plan and execute a wedding."

"Shelby, you're my oldest child. I've dreamed of your wedding since you were a little girl."

"I know, Mama. I'm sorry."

"Is this really what you want, baby?"

"Yes, Mama, it is."

"Then I'll support your decision. The only thing I ask is that you let me be there when you get married."

"Of course, Mama. I wouldn't have it any other way."

Shelby ended the call with her mother and wrapped her arms around Christian. She couldn't believe in less than twenty-four hours, they would officially become Mr. and Mrs. Christian Tyler.

Chapter Forty-One

Christian packed up his belongings and called Daniel over to the apartment. He felt like he hadn't slept a wink all night. The anticipation of making Shelby his wife kept him going. He felt a tinge of guilt for not notifying his mother or best friend of his plans, but he knew it was for the best. Shantrice only knew of his travel plans for his return. She had no idea he had purchased a second ticket for Shelby in the name of Shelby Tyler.

The doorbell rang, and Christian hurried to answer it. He opened the door to find a man, wearing a navy blue suit and holding a clipboard standing outside. The man greeted Christian with a smile.

"Good morning. Mr. Tyler, I presume?" The man asked.

"Yes, I'm Christian Tyler." He replied.

"I'm Lamont with Everyday Car Rentals. I'm here to deliver the car you requested."

"Of course, would you like to come in?"

"Oh, no, Sir. If you don't mind, I would like for you to step outside with me. I need you to inspect the vehicle and sign the paperwork stating I delivered the car to you in a satisfactory manner."

Christian followed Lamont out to the car and examined the vehicle for cleanliness. "Everything looks fine."

"Thank you, Sir. I need you to sign here stating you have inspected the vehicle and are satisfied with the condition.

I also need you to sign in this second box indicating you will be dropping the car of at our Nashville airport location."

Following Lamont's instructions, Christian signed the appropriate places and accepted the keys from him. After shaking his hand, Lamont hopped into a waiting vehicle and left.

Daniel pulled up just as Lamont was leaving. Christian waved at him acknowledging his arrival. He stood and waited for Daniel to park his car and get out. Daniel walked up and greeted Christian with a handshake and a hug. The two went into Christian's apartment.

Taking a seat on the chair, Christian and Daniel talked about the past few months they had worked together. Daniel told him about the outpouring of support from the community for the youth center.

"I tell you, this has truly been a life changing experience for me. I know without a doubt, I was meant to be here," Christian said.

"I believe that too." Daniel replied.

A smile creased Christian's lips as he recalled the excitement of the children and parents as they toured the youth center. Several people had approached him and voiced their appreciation for his work. He knew in his heart; his labor was not in vain.

Christian reached into his pocket and pulled out a set of keys. He extended the keys to Daniel. "Here are the keys to the apartment and the vehicle. I really appreciate you all allowing me to use the vehicle and this apartment. That was much more than I ever expected."

Daniel accepted the keys from Christian. "Man, we were honored to provide you with these things. It was the least we could do. You offered us your services, and expertise, and didn't ask for anything in return. In addition to that, you worked tirelessly on the center from start to finish. Most days you arrived before any of us, and you left after most of us. Words can't express how much we truly appreciate you. Our prayer is that God will bless you abundantly for what you did for the families here in Bethany."

"Thank you, man. That means a lot. I can honestly say, the gift I received here in Bethany was priceless."

A wide grin spread across Christian's face.

"That grin on your face, requires no explanation. I'm happy for you and Shelby. She's a good woman. I'm glad things worked out."

"I have to admit I owe your wife a huge debt of gratitude for opening my eyes."

"I guess sometimes her butting in pays off." Daniel joked.

"I don't know about any other times, but it paid off big time in this case." Christian replied.

Christian looked down at his watch. The time displayed 8:15 am. He and Shelby had agreed to meet at the County Clerk's office at 9:00. She didn't want to ride over together because she wanted him to be surprised at her appearance.

Daniel stood to leave. "I better get out of here. Deborah has a honey do list for me a mile long. If I don't get going now I will never get everything done. You know what they say, happy wife, happy life."

"I hear you, man," Christian said rising to his feet as well. He patted Daniel on the shoulder.

"If it's okay with you, I'll just turn the bottom lock when I leave. I have an appointment this morning that I must keep. I'll be out of here within the hour."

"Man, take your time, that will be fine. I'll call the owner and let him know you're leaving today."

"That'll work. I'll talk to you soon."

Daniel left the apartment and Christian quickly went into the bedroom and changed clothes.

He put on a dark grey single button suit with a white shirt and a burgundy paisley bowtie that he decided to leave open.

He grabbed the rings that he and Shelby had purchased the previous night after she agreed to elope and placed them in his pocket. He slid his feet into his shoes and loaded up the rental car.

One final check of the apartment and he was ready to head to the Clerk's office.

He took out his phone and dialed Shelby's number. She answered on the first ring.

"Good morning, beautiful. Are you as ready to become my wife as I am your husband?"

"I sure am," Shelby purred into the phone. I can't wait to see you. Mama was so excited that she got here at six this morning. She said even though we aren't having a traditional wedding, her daughter was not going to look like something someone threw together. I have a surprise for you, but I won't tell you what it is until I see you."

"Marrying you is all I need."

"Well you're getting that, and according to the clock we only have about thirty minutes. I better go so that I can finish getting ready. I'll see you soon, honey. I love you."

Shelby's words felt like angels singing in his ears. This was really about to happen. Christian jumped in the rental car and headed straight for the clerk's office.

❀❀❀❀

Christian pulled up in front of the clerk's office and parked his vehicle. He waited patiently for Shelby to arrive. His heart started to pound when he saw her car approaching. He noticed her mother was driving. She pulled into an empty slot and turned off the engine. Before Shelby had the opportunity to pull on the handle, Christian was there to open her door.

"You look amazing, my love." He complimented as he took her hand and helped her out of the car.

"You're looking pretty debonair yourself," she replied with a wink.

Christian raised her arm and slowly turned her around taking in the full scope of her beauty. He couldn't believe this beautiful woman was about to become his wife.

Shelby wore a white lace strapless tea length dress and white sandals. She wore her hair pulled over to one side with a blue crystal embellished butterfly pin holding it in place. Diamond studs that her mother loaned her glistened from each ear. A new white gold locket hung from her neck.

Grabbing her by the hand, Christian escorted her into the Clerk's office. He furrowed his eyebrows when he noticed her mother hadn't left the car. She remained seated on the driver's side.

"Why isn't your mother coming in?" he asked with confusion etched over his face.

"You'll see. Come on, let's do this."

The couple walked into the clerk's office and asked for the person in charge of issuing marriage licenses. They were escorted to an office with an older lady seated behind the desk. She extended her arm to them and invited them in.

After a series of questions. Christian and Shelby presented their driver's licenses and social security cards to the lady. Christian paid the required fee and they watched as she printed out their marriage license. Shelby's palms started to sweat. She couldn't believe this was actually happening.

The clerk smiled and extended the license over to them. "When are you planning to wed?" she asked.

"Today. Right now," Christian eagerly blurted out.

"Oh." The woman replied, taken aback. "Will you need the services of our Justice of the peace?"

"Yes," he called out.

"No." Shelby spoke up. "We won't, thank you."

Christian looked at Shelby with disbelief. Sadness immediately filled his eyes.

"What do you mean no?" he asked.

"That's the surprise I was telling you about. Mama stayed outside because she is going to drive to the location where we will be married. We can follow her in your car."

Obvious relief swept over him. The clerk didn't know what to think. She shook each of their hands and offered them her congratulations. She made it a point to tell them their marriage won't be official until they returned the signed license to her office.

"That won't be a problem," Christian spoke up. We'll be back shortly."

He grabbed Shelby by the hand and they walked out of the building together. Once he was outside he pointed to her mother and shook his head.

Linda laughed and started the car.

Shelby stepped aside as Christian opened her door. She slid inside and bounced in her seat.

He got in and turned on the ignition. He leaned over and kissed her passionately.

Linda blew the horn and pointed forward letting him know it was time to go.

Christian followed Linda closely.

He didn't know where they were going but as long as Shelby was sitting next to him, he didn't care.

Ten-minutes later, they arrived at a familiar location.

Standing next to the lake where he and Shelby often spent time together, was a decorated arch and a man, Christian hadn't met before. He noticed a small black book in the man's hand. He turned to Shelby for an explanation.

She was smiling proudly. "When I told Mama about us eloping she said there was no way her baby would get married in a courthouse or judge's office. She called her pastor and asked him to marry us. I don't know where she got the arch from."

They climbed out of the car and headed towards the pastor.

When they got closer, Christian noticed a woman that appeared to be the Pastor's wife standing off in the distance. A wave of guilt swept over him. He knew he should have allowed his mother to participate in his marriage, but he didn't want anyone to talk him out of his desire to marry Shelby.

Standing before the pastor, Christian shook his hand and introduced himself.

Linda continuously snapped pictures with her phone.

He faced Shelby and took her by the hand. He didn't think it was possible for her to be more beautiful than she was at that moment. All reservations were gone. He was ready to make her his wife.

The pastor spoke with eloquence. "We are gathered together in the presence of God to join this man and woman together in holy matrimony."

Shelby gripped Christian's hands tightly. As they made their vows to one another. The love they felt for each other showed in the tone of their voice and the look in their eyes.

Sunlight radiated off the water causing a glow to reflect off the archway. Christian knew he was doing the right thing.

Time seemed to stand still as he heard the pastor make the statement he had been waiting to hear.

"By the power vested in me as a minister of the gospel and by the State of Tennessee. I now pronounce you man and wife. You may kiss your bride."

Christian pulled Shelby into his arms and kissed her like he had never kissed her before.

Epilogue

Shelby held her husband's hand as they prepared to exit the plane. She could not believe how quickly her life had changed. She didn't know what to expect once she stepped off the plane, but she knew there was no turning back. She was officially married.

Christian didn't hesitate to take the signed license back to the Clerk's office. He said when he returned home he wanted to place their official license on the wall.

The airport was extremely busy.

Shelby held on to Christian's arm tightly. He sensed her nervousness and turned to kiss her.

"Don't worry baby, I got you."

She stepped quickly to keep up with him.

They retrieved their bags and noticed a man in a black tuxedo holding a sign that read Mr. and Mrs. Christian Tyler. Christian moved in the direction of the man.

The man waved his hand and another man appeared with a rolling cart. He took the bags from Christian and Shelby and followed them out to the waiting car.

A black suburban with darkly tinted windows was parked outside the airport.

The driver stepped out and opened the door for Christian and Shelby. The man that held the sign for them loaded their bags into the back of the car and bided them farewell.

"My friend, Blake wanted to pick me up but I told him I wasn't coming alone. He works in the entertainment industry so he told me he would send over one of the cars he uses for his celebrity clients. Once Blake gave me the information I called and gave the driver our names for the sign."

She grinned. "Oh so I'm getting celebrity treatment, I see."

"From now until forever, baby. I will always show you how much you mean to me."

The car pulled around the circular driveway stopping in front of Christian's house. The driver opened the door to let them out.

Shelby stepped out of the car and almost fell down. She couldn't believe her eyes. The massive structure that stood before her was stunning. Palm trees surrounded the two story house. The driveway was laid completely in stone. A fountain stood in the center of the driveway. The house was made of dark brown brick, surrounded by large windows.

Christian looked at the smile on her face and knew she was pleased.

He grabbed her by the hand and escorted her to the front door. Turning the key to the lock he picked her up and carried her inside.

"Welcome home, Mrs. Tyler."

"Oh my God, Christian, this is beautiful." Shelby looked at the grand staircase and the large crystal chandelier that hung from the ceiling. Hardwood floors were laid throughout the four thousand square feet structure.

"Let me take you on a tour," Christian offered placing her in a standing position.

He showed her the kitchen with cherry wood cabinets and granite countertops. The formal living room and dining rooms were decorated in modern furnishings. He led her to the guest bedrooms and what he called the downstairs master bedroom on the main level.

Next he took her upstairs to the grand master bedroom. The room was designed like something out of a magazine. A California king size bed was adorned with more pillows than she had ever seen on one bed. The closet was the size of a large bedroom by itself.

"I've been waiting for my bride. This closet is all yours sweetheart. I've been sleeping downstairs but we can move up to this room if you prefer. I want you to be comfortable."

"Baby, this is more than I could have ever imagined." Shelby said.

She laid across the bed and invited her husband to join her.

Kicking off his shoes he quickly complied. Moving into his arms Shelby kissed him. She wanted all of the love she felt for him to radiate from her body to his.

"Christian, where are you? I know you're here because I see your luggage," a woman yelled. "Christian."

Shelby immediately pushed him off of her. "Who is that?"

Jumping up from the bed, Christian straightened his clothes. "It's not what you think, baby. I promise."

"Christian." The woman continued to yell.

"Here I come," he yelled back.

Looking over at his wife, he instructed her to fix her clothes and meet him downstairs.

Giving him a sidelong glance Shelby rolled her eyes and nodded her head in agreement.

Christian descended the stairs and found his mother standing in the living room.

"What on earth are you doing, and why didn't you call and tell me you had arrived home? You got me up in here yelling like somebody that has lost their mind. What were you up there doing anyway?"

Shelby's shoes tapped on the hardwood floor signaling her arrival. Iris spun around and glared at the strange woman standing before her. Christian moved hurriedly and stood by Shelby's side.

He kissed Shelby on the lips, and turned to his mother. "Mom, this is Shelby, my wife."

"*Your what!*" Iris yelled, just before she hit the floor.

The End

Note from the Author

Thank you for taking the time to read my story Journey to Love. I hope you have enjoyed my written work. I count it a blessing to have the gift of writing stories to entertain, encourage, and inspire readers. One thing that I hope you will take away from Journey to Love is encouragement to know that no dream is too big. The things that you desire to happen in your life can and will happen, if you keep the faith and work towards them.

In my story, I named the town Bethany because it reminds me of the Biblical town where siblings Mary, Martha, and Lazarus lived. The situation with Lazarus seemed hopeless until Jesus brought resurrection. Much like the characters in Journey to Love. Christian and Shelby were content with their lives as they were until their unlikely union changed everything.

Upon completion of Journey to Love, I discovered there was in fact an actual town in Tennessee named Bethany. The town in my story is completely fictional and in no way references the actual town of Bethany, Tennessee.

It is my desire to continue to bring you stories that will make an impact on your life in some way. I request your continued support.

About The Author

LaCricia A'ngelle is a licensed Evangelist, Author, and Publisher. A native of Chicago, she currently resides in Georgia with her family. This is her fourth novel.

To arrange signings, book events, speaking engagements, or to send comments to the author please email her at:
author@lacriciaangelle.com

Connect with LaCricia A'ngelle online at:
www.lacriciaangelle.com
www.facebook.com/lacriciaangelle or
www.facebook.com/authorlacricia
Twitter: @authorlacricia
Instagram: @lacricia_angelle

www.ingramcontent.com/pod-product-compliance
Lightning Source LLC
Chambersburg PA
CBHW021950170626
46808CB00001B/96